MISTLETOE MAGIC

A REGENCY ROMANCE

ROSE PEARSON

Home for Christmas

MISTLETOE MAGIC: A REGENCY ROMANCE

Home For Christmas

By

Rose Pearson

HOME FOR CHRISTMAS

...a sweet, romantic journey spanning decades - even centuries - of holiday cheer.

There's no better season than Christmas to look back with gratitude for all the family blessings and forward with anticipation to all the joy to come. A holiday romance or a surprise Christmas wedding that leads to a lifetime of happiness is an irresistible story for a true romantic. Add some snow, hot chocolate, and carols at the piano and you'll fall in love again and again.

Second chances, mail order brides, marriages of convenience – this clean and wholesome series brings all this and so much more. Join our heroes and heroines from proper Regency England to the majestic Rocky Mountains as they find peace, true love, and inspiring Christmas spirit.

This multi-author Christmas series is brought to you by these best-selling authors:

Joyce Alec

Rose Pearson

Natalie Dean

Bethany Rose

Annie Boone

Hanna Hart

Sophie Mays

Home for Christmas Series Page

PROLOGUE

"Georgiana?"

Georgiana, who had been busying herself with her needlework on what was otherwise a very damp and cold winter's day, lifted her head as her brother walked into the drawing-room.

"Ah, Georgiana, there you are," he said, a kind smile on his face and a sharp look in his eyes that sent a twinge of concern into Georgiana's heart. "Might I pry you away from your needlework for a moment?"

Georgiana looked at her brother steadily, taking him in. The Earl had become much more amenable of late, given he had married a little less than a year ago, but with the look in his eye at present, Georgiana felt herself become somewhat unsettled. Something was afoot, and she was not sure she would like whatever it was.

"Georgiana?"

She blinked. "Oh, yes," she said, realizing she had not yet answered the question. "Yes, of course, Allerton."

Setting her needlework on the arm of the chair, she looked up at him expectantly.

"Good." He beamed at her as though he were certain she would be pleased with whatever it was he had to offer her. "You are aware, I hope, of the little Season that is due to start very soon?"

Georgiana frowned. The summer Season had been her third foray into society, for she had made her come out some two years ago but had then been invited to Bath for her second Season by a very close friend of her late mother, Lady Clarence. Her brother had been more than pleased for her to go; it had meant he would have less responsibility and, therefore, more freedom to do as he wished. She had spent the winter with Lord and Lady Clarence, enjoying the little Season, only to hear a very strange rumor being thrown around Bath that the Earl of Allerton was to marry—and to marry soon. What a shock it had been to hear that this rumor was, in fact, nothing short of the truth! At first, she had thought him to be making a mockery of her and thus had not wanted to believe it, but by the time the wedding came around, Georgiana had very little idea *but* to accept that her brother was to marry! Thankfully, his choice of bride had been most excellent indeed, and since that time, Georgiana had found Lady Alice Allerton to be kindness itself. This home had been happier than ever before, and their lives on the estate brought them all some quiet contentment.

It now seemed that this contentedness was to be shattered.

"I have it in my mind to take us all to London!" her

brother exclaimed, throwing up his hands as if excited himself at the prospect. "I know that your summer Season went very well indeed, but since no offers of marriage came to you, I think it best that we return to London for the winter Season also."

Georgiana looked up into her brother's face and felt her stomach tighten. Yes, the summer Season had gone well, but her brother was correct to say she had received no proposals. The gentlemen had been charming enough, and one or two had called on her a good many times, but none had sought to take matters any further. Georgiana had not known why. Was it because she was on her third Season and therefore considered to be almost on the shelf? Or was it because they believed her brother would give her no great dowry, given he had married Alice for her wealth?

"What say you, Georgiana?" her brother asked, beaming at her as though she ought to be practically dancing around the room in joy. "We shall once again go to London, and you shall have another opportunity to find a suitable match."

Georgiana bit her lip. "Brother, whilst I am truly grateful to you for your willingness to aid me in this matter, I fear it will be of no use."

Lord Allerton's face darkened, the smile fading away and his eyes losing some of their brightness. "What can you mean?"

"Well," Georgiana said, speaking in very practical terms. "I have been in London for two summer Seasons and in Bath for one, but as yet, I have not found a single gentleman to seek my hand in marriage. I fear," she continued, forcing her own emotions down so she could speak without her voice shaking or her eyes filling with tears. "I fear it might be quite impossible for me to do so even during the little Season, Allerton. I am perhaps now considered to be 'on the shelf,' or mayhap there is a worry that my dowry might be a good deal smaller than what a gentleman would expect." She dropped her eyes from her brother's face, seeing his sharp look and not wanting him to feel any guilt over what she was saying. "I fear that another Season will not bring about what you expect."

There was silence for some time. Georgiana did not know where to look, her heart aching as she let her gaze drift around the room. When she finally dared a glance at her brother, she saw that his brows were low over his eyes and that his expression was shuttered. She could not tell what he was feeling, praying he did not think she was attempting to blame him in any way for her present unmarried state. Dropping her head, Georgiana pressed her lips together tightly, wondering if she should say anything more.

"I have it!"

Her breath caught as she shot a look up to her brother who was, much to her astonishment, now grinning from ear to ear.

"Allerton?" she queried slowly, butterflies beginning to beat their wings furiously in the pit of her stomach. "What is it?"

"I have it," he said again, coming towards her and crouching down so he might look up into her face. His hand found hers, and he squeezed her fingers tightly. "You have every right to worry," he continued as she swallowed hard. "It is not because you are not lovely in every way that the gentlemen do not wish to draw near to you, but rather because your foolish brother has yet to prove himself."

Georgiana's mouth hung open for a moment, astonished that her brother had accepted such a responsibility so quickly. That was most unlike him—but, then again, he had changed significantly in almost every way since he had married Alice Jones.

"Therefore," her brother continued, his smile gentle, "therefore, you need not worry you will find no one to court you. *I* will do so on your behalf."

Something kicked hard at Georgiana's stomach. "What do you mean?" she asked quickly as her brother rose to his feet, smiling at her fondly. "What are your intentions, Allerton?"

He shrugged. "I will find you a suitable match, Georgiana, just as I arranged my match with Alice. That has turned out wonderfully well, you must admit, and I can only hope you will find a similar happiness with whomever it is that I choose for you."

Georgiana tried to say something in response, tried to open her mouth to protest that her brother did not need to go to such lengths, only to find that her lips were refusing to do as she intended. Allerton's smile remained on his face, his expression warm as he gave a contented sigh.

"I will ensure to consider at length the many gentlemen that might suit you," he said in a clear attempt to reassure her. "I will not be hasty nor will I simply make a match in order to suit myself. You need have no fear of that, my dear sister. I am not that sort of gentleman any longer, thanks to Alice."

"I know that to be true," Georgiana answered, surprised at just how thin her voice was, how tight her throat felt. "I will make sure to thank her also." She did not know what else to say, feeling as though she were being swept along in a fast-flowing river without any means of escape. Her brother was trying to do his best for her, she knew, but she had never wanted him to find her a match! She had enjoyed being able to meet and converse with the various gentlemen of the *ton,* although it had been a great disappointment when none of them had sought to take matters any further with her.

She smiled at her brother as he took his leave, giving her the day of their departure for London, but the smile did not speak of any true joy or happiness in her heart. Instead, she felt nothing more than fear and worry.

"I will let you return to your needlework," Lord Allerton said, reaching down to pat Georgiana's hand. "You need not look so fearful, my dear sister. It will all turn out very well indeed. I am sure of it."

"I thank you," Georgiana murmured as her brother walked from the room, feeling a sense of relief cloak her as the door closed. In the silence that followed, Georgiana was left with a myriad of thoughts and emotions, leaving her feeling quite overwhelmed.

"It may not be as bad as you fear," she told herself aloud, forcibly stemming the flood of tears that poured into her eyes. "You need not be afraid."

Georgiana swallowed hard, forcing her tears back and looking up the ceiling in an attempt to keep them at bay. Her brother *had* changed over this last year, and she was sure he would not make a match for her without asking for Alice's opinion—and Lady Allerton was both wise and considerate. And did she herself not want to marry? She had always longed for a husband and a home of her own, for that was every young lady's dream. That dream had felt very far away of late, but now, mayhap, it would be fulfilled, even if she herself had not made the choice of who to marry. She had seen plenty of marriages of convenience, plenty young ladies thrown into their future without any consideration for their feelings on the matter, and she ought to be grateful that her brother would not be that way inclined. He would be careful, considerate, and, hopefully, wise in his choice.

All she had to do was prepare herself to meet her future husband, no matter who he might be.

CHAPTER ONE

"And here we are."

Georgiana pressed her hands together as she held them in her lap, looking out of the window as though seeing the townhouse would help her calm her nerves. She threw a quick glance towards her sister-in-law, seeing how Lady Allerton smiled back at her without any worry in her eyes. That was how Georgiana wished to be: free of all anxiety and, therefore, happy, contented and settled.

It was not how she felt at present.

"Your brother will do all he can to help find you a suitable match, Georgiana." Alice's voice, lilting with the American accent that had taken Georgiana some time to become used to. "But I will be here too. You know that, I hope."

"I do, of course," Georgiana answered, seeing the kindness in Lady Allerton's smile and feeling it soothe her fractious thoughts. "I would be glad for your input when it comes to my brother's decisions, Alice. He may well choose someone he believes will be entirely suitable and, whilst they will appear to be so with their good title, excellent fortune, and perfect family line, they might fall short in their character."

"Which I quite understand," Lady Allerton said with a small sigh and a slight shake of her head that betrayed just how well she understood Georgiana's dilemma. "Your brother has a good heart, Georgiana. He means well, but his considerations do not always have much of an...emotive nature. As you have just said, he thinks mostly of family lines, of titles and wealth."

"Which mean very little," Georgiana muttered, sitting back in her carriage seat and sighing heavily. "Although I should not wish to marry a pauper."

"No, indeed not," Lady Allerton chuckled as the carriage came to a stop. "That would cause a good many difficulties indeed!"

Georgiana sighed again, shivering just a little as the carriage door was opened. The drive to London had taken some time, and even with the hot bricks, their multiple blankets, and their many stops, it was still cold in the carriage. She would be glad to get inside and to sit in front of a roaring fire for a time.

Once inside, Georgiana threw aside any suggestion of resting in her bedchamber and made her way directly to the drawing-room. Her brother had ridden to London a day earlier than they and had ensured the house was prepared for their arrival. There was a warm fire waiting for her in the drawing-room and Georgiana hurried towards it, her hands outstretched and desperate for the warmth.

"Ah, Georgiana, there you are!"

She let out a small shriek, spinning around to see her brother sitting in an armchair close to the fire. He chuckled good-naturedly, getting up out of his chair and making for the door, ready to greet his wife.

"I did not see you there," she stammered as he grinned. "You arrived safely, then?"

"I did," he said just as Lady Allerton came into the room. "And here is my dear wife." Embracing her warmly, Georgiana looked away, a little embarrassed to be watching such a display of affection, and yet, at the same time, there came a pang of longing. A longing she too might find such happiness and love for herself. Her brother and Alice's marriage had been one of arrangement, not one that had come from any sort of emotion yet, a love had been borne from it. A love that was evident every day. That was the sort of love Georgiana wanted for herself—and just because her marriage would be one of arrangement did not mean there was no chance for such a thing to occur.

"You will be glad to know, Georgiana, that I have already found two suitable gentlemen for you to meet," her brother said, drawing Lady Allerton along with him as he walked back towards the center of the room. "I am sure you will think very highly of them both."

Georgiana exchanged a quick glance with Lady Allerton before smiling at her brother. "I thank you," she told him with as much fervor as she could manage. "You have been working hard on my behalf, and I am truly grateful." Seeing how her brother smiled, she spread out her hands in a questioning gesture. "Might I inquire as to their names?"

"But of course!" Lord Allerton exclaimed as the door opened to allow in two maids who set down trays of refreshments and a slightly steaming pot of tea that caught both Georgiana and Lady Allerton's eye almost at once. "One is Lord Tolliver, who is a Viscount with excellent holdings, whilst the other is the Earl of Pembrokeshire."

Lady Allerton frowned. "The Earl of Pembrokeshire?" she repeated as her husband nodded fervently. "Is he not the very same gentleman who had to deal with the consequences of what was a terrible scandal in the summer?"

Georgiana's stomach dropped to the floor as she looked at her brother, seeing how he winced.

"He is the very same," he admitted to his wife. "I have to speak to him about that particular matter and, of course, if I find such a thing to be true, then there will be no—"

"Allerton!" Lady Allerton was staring at her husband, her eyes flashing and one hand curled into a fist. "You cannot push your poor sister towards a gentleman who has been accused of attempting to elope with the daughter of a Duke simply so he might find a little more financial stability in the long term."

Georgiana's eyes flared wide as she looked from her brother to Lady Allerton and back again. Had her brother honestly thought that such a gentleman would be suitable for her?

"There may be no truth to it," Lord Allerton said

hastily, holding up his hands defensively. "I will speak to Lord Pembrokeshire and discover whether or not it has even a small hint of truth about it."

"And if it does?" Lady Allerton demanded, sounding quite upset with her husband. "What then?"

Lord Allerton began to stammer, and Georgiana could not help but smile. It seemed her brother was not going to be able to make any foolish decisions given the strength of his wife, and for that, she was very glad indeed.

"Of course, I shall not make any agreement with Lord Pembrokeshire if I discover those rumors to have any basis in truth," he said firmly, which only took a little fire from Lady Allerton's eyes. "You need not worry, my dear. I shall be very careful indeed."

Lady Allerton sniffed, lifted her chin, and fixed her husband with an icy gaze. "Be sure you are," she told him, sternly, as Georgiana watched with a mixture of both amusement and relief. "For I shall not permit Georgiana to marry anyone with such a reputation."

Lord Allerton cleared his throat, gesturing for them all to sit down. Lady Allerton poured the tea, handing Georgiana a cup before sitting down herself and looking expectantly at her husband, clearly thinking he had more to say.

"You will need some new gowns, of course," Lord Allerton said as Georgiana nodded eagerly. "The winter is to be a very cold one indeed, or so I am told, although the frost has not been lingering for too much of the day as yet."

Georgiana nodded, sipping her tea and closing her

eyes at the wonderful warmth that began to spread through her. After the long and arduous journey in the cold carriage, she finally felt as though she were becoming warm again. "I thank you, Allerton," she told her brother. "I will need a new cloak also, I believe, not because there is any need for me to cling to the latest fashions, but merely because I—"

"You shall have whatever you please for whatever reason you may want it," her brother interrupted with a charming smile in her direction as if he were trying to make up for his foolishness only some moments before. "You know very well that things are much improved when it comes to financial matters, and thus, I am very happy indeed to pay for whatever you require."

A sudden urge to go out into London again hit Georgiana hard and, as she sipped her tea again, she glanced towards Lady Allerton. The lady herself might be too tired to join her, but surely there was a maid she could take as a chaperone?

"Might I go to a few shops this afternoon?" she asked, making her brother look up in surprise. "I know we have only just arrived, and there cannot be long until the dark evenings begin to creep in on us, but I should very much like to take a stroll through London."

Her brother made to shake his head, only to catch a sharp glance from his wife. "I—yes, of course," he stammered a little awkwardly. "I will attend with you, shall I? Not that I have any intention of looking at ribbons or the like, but rather that I would walk with you if you would wish it. Although I would prefer to take the carriage, of course."

"Then the carriage it shall be," Georgiana shrugged, thinking to herself she would not mind taking the carriage if it meant she could wander in and out of the shops that offered so many wonderful things. "Shall we say, within the hour?"

Her brother sighed heavily, although a teasing smile caught the corner of his mouth. "Within the hour," he agreed, finally managing to earn a warm look from his wife, which seemed to please him greatly. "And we will ensure to purchase you a new cloak at least, for you cannot go about London without such a thing."

"I will make sure to do so," Georgiana answered, setting her teacup down and rising to her feet. "If you will excuse me, I will go to prepare for our departure."

The London shops were everything Georgiana remembered them to be, although the damp, cold weather did seem to lessen their appeal just a little. In the summertime, one could walk along the street and see windows covered in bright colors, with ribbons displayed in one window and a new bonnet in another. Now, however, in the gloom of the day, it felt as though there were a drabness to the ribbons and a dullness to the bonnets that had not been there before. But Georgiana felt quite contented in herself regardless, smiling warmly at every shopkeeper she saw.

A new cloak was purchased without too much difficulty, and Georgiana knew it would keep her very warm indeed. She purchased a new muffler in another shop and then some ribbons in the third. The gowns and the like would have to wait until another day, of course, but the joy of being back in London again filled Georgiana's soul, even when it began to rain.

"The carriage is a little away still, my dear," her brother said, looking glumly up at the sky. "We might go into this bookshop for a moment until the rain begins to lessen?"

A sudden thundering caught Georgiana unexpectedly, making her gasp in fright as the sound rolled across the sky, making everything else fall entirely silent. It faded away completely, only for the skies to open and the rain to pour with such intensity that Georgiana felt it soaking through her bonnet almost at once.

Her brother did not hesitate but practically pushed her in through the door of the bookshop, hurrying in himself after her. A flash of lightning lit up the sky, making her gasp with fright as she pressed both hands to her hammering heart, feeling both awestruck and afraid in equal measure.

"Good afternoon," she heard her brother say, turning her head to see him speak to the proprietor. "We will have to linger in your shop a while, I fear, but I will make sure to purchase a few books from you."

The proprietor did not look to be at all disturbed by this remark, inclining his head towards Lord Allerton. "But of course," came the reply. "You must wait for as long as is necessary. This thunder should pass soon, I'd expect, but the rain..." he trailed off, and Georgiana looked back out of the window, seeing how the rain practically bounced off the pavement and the cobbles of the street. It was quite a downpour!

"You must find at least one book to purchase, Georgiana," her brother said, his voice low as he came towards her. "It is only fair."

She laughed, the fear and unease of the thunderstorm finally fading away. "I can find more than one," she told him teasingly. "I will have at least five by the time our carriage arrives and the rain has died away."

Her brother arched one eyebrow, but Georgiana laughed and turned away, letting her eyes drift along the stacked shelves of books in the hope she might find a new novel of some kind with which she might occupy herself for a time. She was not a great reader by any means, which, most likely, her brother knew, but she would certainly be able to pull out a few books to purchase to take home. The winter meant there were undoubtedly fewer afternoon calls and the like that would entertain her, so she might perhaps finish even three novels by the time Christmas came.

Her heart lifted at the thought of Christmas. She had already enjoyed one Christmas with her brother and his new wife, and it had been such a wonderful occasion, she was looking forward to this year with an even greater sense of anticipation. There would be the singing of carols, the greenery brought into the house, the mistletoe and the holly berries that made her heart swell with the sheer joy of the Christmas season. There would be gifts to give and celebrations to enjoy. Georgiana was quite certain it would be just as lovely as the previous year... although whether or not she would be engaged by then, she had very little idea. There was only one month until Christmas Day, but that was long enough for her brother to make an agreement with whatever gentleman he settled on.

Just so long as it is not Lord Pembrokeshire, she thought to herself, grimly. *Even Alice knows he is not suitable!*

Another thunderclap caught her off guard, making her jump as a small exclamation left her mouth. A little embarrassed, she clamped one hand over her mouth, praying that no one had heard her.

"I was a little frightened too."

Her cheeks heated furiously as she turned her head to see a gentleman looking at her, a small smile lifting his mouth as his eyes fixed on her. He was standing a short distance away, at the end of a shelf of books, and as she watched him, he came around to her, drawing a little closer. Her heart squeezed tight for a moment, realizing she did not know this gentleman and, as such, she should not engage with him.

"Are you hiding from the rain?" the gentleman asked, his accent capturing her attention. "I confess I'm having to do the same."

"You...you are from America," Georgiana said before realizing what she was saying. Flushed, she dropped her head. "Forgive me," she stammered, daring a glance up at the gentleman. "I did not mean to—"

"Please, please." The gentleman was chuckling, his hands held up. "You needn't worry. But yes, you are correct. I am from Boston." He bowed deeply. "Mr. Oliver Lowell."

Georgiana dipped into a curtsy, aware her cheeks were still a little red. This was not at all the correct procedure, and certainly her brother would think her very improper to be continuing to converse with a gentleman who had not yet been properly introduced to her but, given the circumstances, and given he was from an entirely different country, Georgiana decided to continue as she was.

"I am glad to make your acquaintance," she said quietly, a little relieved the sound of the rain on the roof quietened her voice all the more. "I am Lady Georgiana, sister to the Earl of Allerton."

The gentleman blinked in surprise, perhaps unused to such high titles. "I see," he said after a moment. "Well, Lady Georgiana, I hope to see you again while I'm here in London. I came to visit a cousin and should be here for a few weeks still." A shoulder lifted in a half shrug. "I haven't decided if I'll stay here for Christmas or not. I guess I'll have to wait and see how things go."

Georgiana, unused to having a stranger speak so openly to her, smiled a little cautiously, taking the gentleman in. He was not overly tall, although half a head taller than herself, with a broad frame and a thick head of dark brown hair. His appearance was pleasing, with hazel eyes, ruddy cheeks, and a lopsided smile that seemed to add to his charm. His speech, however, was very dissimilar to that of the *ton,* and his manner, of course, was certainly very different to what she might expect. Not that she held it against him, of course, for she knew very well just how difficult it had been for her sister-in-law.

"I hail from Boston," he continued, making Georgiana realize there had been a silence for a moment or two that had added a slight sense of strain between them. "Although my cousin removed here a few years ago."

"I see," Georgiana answered, politely. "My brother recently married, and his wife comes from America also." She smiled as his expression became one of astonishment. "That is why I recognized your accent."

Mr. Lowell blinked rapidly, then shook his head in evident surprise. "Well, that's wonderful to hear, Lady Georgiana," he said. "It can be difficult to fit into London society, but if your sister-in-law has managed to do so, then I must hope that I will be welcomed also."

"I am sure you will be," she answered with a quick smile. "Might I inquire as to the name of your cousin?"

"Oh, yes, of course. She is Lady Rutledge, married to Viscount Rutledge. They have an estate but they do spend a considerable time here in London."

"Oh." Georgiana searched her memory to see if she had ever been introduced to Lord and Lady Rutledge but found she could not recall their names nor their faces. "I hope to meet them during the little Season, then," she said, covering her lack of knowledge of them. "And I am sure you will find yourself warmly welcomed into society also." Knowing it was time for her to remove herself from the conversation for propriety's sake, she inclined her head and took a step away from him, seeing out of the corner of her eye how he bowed and then turned away. At least he understood certain manners expected within society, she thought to herself, seeing how her brother emerged from another part of the bookshop, one book in his hand.

"You have nothing to read!" he exclaimed, mockingly exasperated. "I thought you were to take five!"

She rolled her eyes at him. "I thought to ask the proprietor to find me a new novel or two," she answered by way of excuse. "I shall do precisely that, should you be willing to wait for a few minutes?"

Lord Allerton sighed heavily, although his eyes twinkled. "Do be quick, Georgiana. The rain is beginning to lessen, and I would like to make for the carriage before it begins to pour again."

"Of course." She smiled and hurried towards the counter, seeing the proprietor looking up at her expectantly. She would have to tell Lady Allerton of her new acquaintance once she returned home. No doubt there would be a good many questions about him, and mayhap Lady Allerton herself would be glad to be introduced to Mr. Lowell. It might bring her some happiness to speak to a fellow countryman.

Thus contented, Georgiana allowed the proprietor to find her not one, but two new novels, her thoughts entirely on the task at hand and no longer settled on her new acquaintance, Mr. Lowell. Although she did not know the same could not be said for him.

CHAPTER TWO

*O*liver could not help but watch the lovely young lady hurry from the bookshop, seeing what he presumed was a footman hurrying from the carriage with an umbrella held out for her. The rain had become a drizzle in the last few minutes, and both she and the gentleman she had been with had taken the chance to hurry to the carriage. He chuckled to himself, turning around as the carriage rolled away. She had been very lovely indeed, but he certainly had surprised her in some way or another.

Quite what he had done, he did not know, but there were certainly a good many aspects of London society he had not yet quite grasped. The news that there was another American here in London brought a fresh sense of happiness to his heart, for whilst he had been enjoying his time here, it did bring with it a small loneliness that often pervaded his otherwise contented life. His cousin and her husband had been more than welcoming and, whilst he had not yet attended any large social gatherings, there had been a small dinner and another soiree he had enjoyed, and he had been to the theatre twice so far. Margaret, his cousin, had been very glad to see him and had gently guided him forward when he had mis-stepped, whilst her husband had merely waved a hand and told Oliver not to worry.

Oliver could not help but look forward to his first London ball, given he had never attended such a thing before. It was to be tomorrow evening, if he recalled correctly, and he could not help but feel a small twinge of excitement as he considered it. Would Lady Georgiana be there? Would he have the opportunity to dance with her? Oliver was not quite sure what to do when it came to dancing, or even how to ask a lady to dance with him, but one thing was for certain—he intended to speak to Lady Georgiana again.

"Are you purchasing these, sir?"

Oliver set down the first three books on the counter and smiled at the proprietor, who looked at him quizzically.

"I would like to," he said with a grin, "but I wonder if you can tell me what sort of book that young lady might like."

The older man blinked slowly, tilting his head just a little to one side. "Young lady, sir?"

"The one who just left," Oliver said gesturing towards the door as though that would remind the fellow. "Lady Georgiana, I think. She was with a gentle-man." He looked back at the proprietor, aware of the slightly wary look in his eyes. Was he doing something wrong?

"You are speaking of Lady Georgiana," the proprietor said slowly. "She was with Lord Allerton, her brother."

Oliver nodded, a little cheered by the proprietor's seeming willingness to continue the conversation. "I should like to know what sort of book she would like," he said, wondering if he was making himself unclear in any way. "She was very kind to me and has informed me that her sister-in-law is also from America, as I am." He shrugged as the proprietor nodded slowly. "I'd like to send her a book that I hope she will enjoy, just as a gesture of thanks."

A look of understanding flooded the proprietor's face, and his smile spread, making Oliver sigh with relief.

"Ah, I quite understand, sir," the man answered, now looking quite happy to help Oliver with his intentions. "It is a very kind gesture, I am sure, and I know she will appreciate it. I helped her to find one or two new books just before she left, so if you wish, I could find another book of the same kind?"

Oliver nodded, leaning one elbow on the counter. "Please," he said gesturing to the bookshelves with his other hand. "That would be very helpful indeed." He smiled to himself as the proprietor hurried off, murmuring under his breath as he went.

At least that is one thing I have managed to do correctly, he thought to himself as the proprietor continued to scurry here and there between the shelves of books. *Sending a book to a lady as a gesture of thanks is obviously quite well thought of!* His broad smile remained as the proprietor came back to the counter with three books in his hands. He laid them out for Oliver to peruse, telling him these were some of the newer novels, and he was sure the lady would be glad to have any of them.

"Send all of them!" Oliver exclaimed on a whim, thinking he would make himself very proper indeed if he were to send three instead of one. "That way she will know just how thankful I am to have met her."

The proprietor goggled at him for a moment, looking at him in evident confusion before shaking his head and muttering to himself under his breath. Oliver frowned, wondering if he had been overeager, only to shrug inwardly and turn his head away. He was merely expressing his thankfulness through a kind gesture, and surely there was nothing that could be said about that!

"I shall have them sent directly," the proprietor said, glancing outside at the rain. "Just as soon as the rain has stopped, so the books do not get damaged."

Oliver nodded in understanding. "Thank you," he said. "I shall pay you and then be on my way."

When Oliver got back to the house, the rain had finally stopped, and the sun was attempting to shine through the clouds, although Oliver was not sure it would last.

"Good gracious!" his cousin cried as he stepped into the house. "Whatever happened to you?"

Oliver looked down at himself, seeing the glistening beads of rain running down his coat. "I am a little damp," he said with a shrug. "The hackneys were hard to find."

Lady Rutledge rolled her eyes. "They are not at all hard to find," she said with a shake of her head. "You need only wave a hand, and one will come to you."

"They were entirely absent from the street!" he protested, handing his hat and gloves to the waiting butler whilst his cousin wrinkled her nose at the water that sprinkled from him as he took off his coat. "I tried my best, of course. I just hope the books I have sent to a lady will have been delivered to her without any difficulty."

His cousin, who had been about to walk away, stopped and turned to face him again. Her dark hair was pulled neatly back from her face, a few ringlet curls around her ears, but her brown eyes were wide with surprise, her mouth a perfect circle.

"What's wrong?" he asked, coming towards her and letting a grin settle on his face. "Is there something the matter?"

Lady Rutledge blinked rapidly, her lips pressing together tightly for a moment. "You sent a book to a lady?" she asked quietly, sounding a little surprised. "To whom?"

He shrugged, not wanting to make much of it. "I met a lady in the bookshop and she spoke very kindly to me. I have even discovered she has a sister-in-law from America!" This exclamation was met with a swift intake of breath, although Oliver did not know why such a thing should distress his cousin so. "Lady Georgiana, if I remember correctly. As a gesture of my thanks for her kindness today, I sent her three books."

A squeak came from his cousin's mouth. "Three?" she whispered, one hand pressed to her mouth, the word muffled behind her fingers. "You sent Lady Georgiana *three* books?"

"Yes," he said a little confused. "Whatever is wrong with that?"

Lady Rutledge closed her eyes tightly, her breathing still obviously a little quick. "Pray tell me how you came to be acquainted with her."

"I—I introduced myself to her," Oliver said as Lady Rutledge let out another exclamation of evident horror. "Why? Whatever is the matter?"

Lady Rutledge let out a long, slow breath and opened her eyes. "My dear cousin, how many times must I tell you that things are very different here in London?"

"You have told me many times," he admitted with a shrug. "But I cannot see what I have done now that is so intolerable."

"You do not introduce yourself to a complete stranger, especially if she is a young lady!" Lady Rutledge cried, throwing her hands up in evident exasperation. "I am sure I have told you such a thing before!"

Oliver shook his head slowly. "No, you haven't," he said firmly. "You or your husband have always been the ones to make the introductions, but I have never known that I should not introduce myself otherwise."

Her face began to turn a dusky shade of pink as Lady Rutledge groaned loudly. "I am sure I have done so," she said firmly. "But not only that, one does not send *three* books to a young lady so soon after their first meeting!"

Growing all the more frustrated, Oliver shook his head in exasperation. "Why does the number of books make any difference?" he asked, wishing he could throw up his hands as she had done. "I wanted to express my thanks at her kindness and for the happiness that was brought by her telling me of her sister-in-law. I cannot see what the problem was with me doing that!"

"Because *one* would have been appropriate!" Lady Rutledge cried, clearly very upset. "One book, one gift, one expression of thanks. Three books is much too overt, Lowell! It will suggest to her much more than a simple thanks."

Oliver swallowed hard, a cold hand grasping his heart. "What do you mean?"

"She will think you are interested in furthering your acquaintance with her!"

"But I am," he said a little confused. "I would very much like to speak to her again. I was hoping she would be willing to dance with me at the ball tomorrow evening."

Lady Rutledge groaned again and put her head in her hands. "You do not understand," she said as though Oliver did not know that already. "To send three books suggests a fondness, Lowell. A regard for her—and not only is such a thing inappropriate for someone you have only just met, but it is highly unorthodox."

Pressing his lips together hard, Oliver let out a long, heavy sigh and tried not to let this sudden uncomfortable sensation overwhelm him. He had never once thought that a gift of three books would suggest anything other than thanks, but now, it seemed, it would say far too much to Lady Georgiana.

"And you cannot simply go up to her and ask her to dance with you at the ball," Lady Rutledge continued in a warning voice. "You must be properly introduced, both to Lady Georgiana and then to Lord and Lady Allerton before you can even *think* of asking to sign her dance card, Lowell."

Sighing heavily, Oliver admitted defeat. "Very well," he said heavily, aware of the large space in between his standing in society and that of Lady Georgiana. "So you are suggesting that I might not be able to dance with her, then."

"I cannot say," Lady Rutledge muttered with a shake of her head. "After what you have done thus far, I cannot pretend the lady herself, as well as Lord Allerton, will not be affected by it. They might consider you to be a little too improper for their acquaintance."

Closing his eyes, Oliver felt a rush of homesickness overtake him. He wanted to return to the life he understood and to the customs that were entirely familiar to him. He had been in London for a few weeks now, and whilst he enjoyed many things there, the expectations and the demands of society were something he could not quite grasp.

"Do not think too much on it," Lady Rutledge said, stepping forward to put one hand on his arm as her eyes shone with a sudden sympathy, perhaps realizing she had been a little too harsh. "I should not have railed at you so. I know you were only trying to express thankfulness to Lady Georgiana, and I am glad she has spoken to you of her sister-in-law."

Oliver swallowed hard, feeling more foolish than ever before. "I would like to be introduced to Lady Allerton still," he told his cousin, seeing how she nodded. "If she refuses my acquaintance, then so be it, but given she is from the same country as I, then I can only hope she will forgive me."

Lady Rutledge smiled tightly but nodded. "I am sure she will understand," she said with more warmth in her voice. "Lady Allerton made quite a stir when she first appeared in London. She knows how difficult it can be. I think, despite what I have said at first, you will have nothing to fear."

A little relieved, Oliver nodded, patted his cousin's hand, and let out a long, heavy breath. "I thank you," he said, using the words that his cousin had taught him to say instead of a simple 'thanks.' "I don't mean to embarrass you in any way. I am sorry if I've managed to do that inadvertently."

Lady Rutledge sighed, but her smile remained intact. "We will manage, I am quite sure," she said with a wry look in her eyes. "Just ensure you stay close to myself or Lord Rutledge tomorrow evening. That way, we should be able to make quite certain you do nothing to shock the *beau monde*." A quiet laugh escaped her as she pressed his arm for a moment and then turned away. "Come, let us take some refreshment in the drawing-room. You will need something warm to drink after being in that downpour, and I certainly could do with a refreshing cup of tea."

Grateful to her for her kindness, Oliver followed without question, praying silently that Lady Georgiana would think just as well of him despite his mistake. The ball no longer held the same sense of appeal; the thought of being in her company again no longer as delightful. He swallowed hard as he walked into the drawing-room, feeling a sense of embarrassment capture him all over again. Hopefully, it would have faded by tomorrow evening, else Oliver was not at all sure how he would manage to make it through the evening! The last thing he wanted was to rush away in a flurry of shame and ruin his standing—as little as it was—within London society.

I will make sure to stick by Lady Rutledge, he told himself as she asked him to ring the bell for tea. *And then surely, nothing else will go wrong!*

CHAPTER THREE

"*D*o you think he will be here this evening?"

Georgiana resisted the urge to roll her eyes at Alice's question, seeing how Lady Allerton looked about the ballroom eagerly. She had been thrilled to hear of Georgiana's meeting with this new gentleman here in London, although Lord Allerton had not been at all pleased to hear that Georgiana had spoken to a gentleman she did not know without any proper introduction. However, Alice had set his mind to rest very easily but, when Lord Allerton was not listening, teased Georgiana relentlessly about Mr. Lowell's eagerness to prove his regard for her.

It had been made all the worse by the appearance of not one, not two, but three books sent by the proprietor of the bookshop where she had met Mr. Lowell, with a short note stating it was from the gentleman as a gesture of thanks. She had not known what to make of it, for whilst it was very kind of him to send her a gift, three books spoke of a fondness for her, which certainly could not be given she was only just acquainted with him! Whilst Lady Allerton had laughed aloud at the gift, telling Georgiana it was most likely a mistake on his part, Lord Allerton had not found it at all humorous. In fact, he had gone out of his way to tell Georgiana that to even *consider* such a gentleman was entirely out of the question.

Georgiana had laughed at this remark, whilst Lady Allerton's color had heightened, and her temper flared at once. Georgiana left the room long before her brother and his wife could begin to argue in earnest, but she knew very well that her brother's statement remained regardless. She had no concern as to her consideration of Mr. Lowell, for given he held no title and would soon be returning to America, she knew it would be foolish indeed to give him even a second thought.

Although she would have to thank him for the books, she realized, closing her eyes for a moment in frustration. Just so long as she was able to do so without anyone over-hearing her, for fear the gossip mongers would set upon her and spread word about herself and Mr. Lowell throughout London.

"Ah."

Georgiana caught herself, looking up to see Alice looking across the ballroom floor, her brows beginning to knit together. "What is it?" she asked, a knot of nerves beginning to tighten in her belly. "Is something wrong?"

"I..." Lady Allerton trailed off, her lips twisting together for a moment before she shot Georgiana a rueful look. "I believe your brother is coming to introduce you to the first of his suggestions."

"Suggestions?" Georgiana repeated, only to realize

what Alice meant. Her eyes sought her brother, eventually finding him in the crowd, seeing him walking towards her purposefully with a gentleman just a step or two behind him.

Surely this could not be the Earl of Pembrokeshire! After the clear concern that Lady Allerton had expressed about him, surely Lord Allerton would not bring him to Georgiana now for an introduction? Or was this, in fact, Lord Tolliver, the viscount her brother had mentioned?

Her stomach dropped to the floor as her brother stepped to one side only to reveal a tall, thin gentleman with a gaunt face and a long broad nose that seemed quite out of place given the rest of his angular features. He was very tall, she realized, seeing him practically looming over her brother. There was no smile on his face as he stopped in front of her, and even his bow was short and sharp. Georgiana tried her best not to stare at her brother as Lord Allerton made the introductions, trying her best to remain as calm and as polite as always.

"Good evening, Lord Tolliver," she said as he looked her up and down in a most improper manner. "I hope you are enjoying this evening?"

"No." The man's voice was grating and harsh. "It is most disagreeable to have to come to London this time of year. The only reason I must do so is because my mother will not stop speaking to me of my lack of marriage partner. And thus," he continued, with a small sniff, "I look to you, Lady Georgiana."

Georgiana stared at Lord Tolliver for a moment or two, dumbstruck by his words and his manner. Her eyes shifted towards her brother who, thankfully, was no longer smiling but looked a little horrified, looking at Lord Tolliver with the same astonished expression that Georgiana was sure was on her face. The silence stretched between them for some moments, with Lord Tolliver never once lifting his eyes from Georgiana, his expectation she would answer more than clear. Georgiana did not know what to say. She could not imagine being wed to such a man, for his manner was not only incredibly brash and rude, but he had embarrassed both himself and her and yet seemed to be entirely unaware of it.

"I think, Lord Tolliver, you have misunderstood me." Georgiana looked across at her brother, whose face had darkened just a little, evidencing his evident upset with Lord Tolliver's words. "I thought to introduce you to my sister, for whilst she needs a husband, I have not yet decided which gentleman would be the most suitable for her."

Lord Tolliver, however, did not seem at all put off by this remark and instead snorted in a most disparaging manner.

"I hardly think you need to concern yourself with suitability," he laughed as though Lord Allerton was being more than a little foolish in showing consideration for Georgiana's requirements. "Any husband will do for your sister, Lord Allerton, provided they are wealthy and bear a good title. I can assure you that I fulfill both of those requirements."

Georgiana shook her head in astonishment and turned her head to see Lady Allerton glaring furiously at Lord Tolliver, her hands planted on her hips and her cheeks a fiery red. Georgiana feared she was about to explode with anger, about to rail at Lord Tolliver without any consideration of what she was saying or who might hear her words, and so she reached out one hand and settled it on Lady Allerton's shoulder.

Lady Allerton jerked visibly, only to let her gaze fall to Georgiana's face, her cheeks still red with evident anger.

"Shall we take a turn about the room?" Georgiana asked whilst Lord Tolliver made a noise of evident disbelief at Georgiana's rudeness. "I feel quite in need of it, do you not?"

Lady Allerton closed her eyes for a moment, then nodded. "I do," she answered, her voice tight. "Shall we depart at this very moment?" She did not wait for Georgiana to answer but stepped forward and took Georgiana's arm in her own, turning them both away from Lord Tolliver and Lord Allerton, both of whom were left standing watching after them, although one with an air of dismay that spoke of the knowledge of just how his wife would berate him once he returned home with her that evening.

"I do not know *what* Allerton is thinking," Lady Allerton hissed as she half dragged Georgiana beside her. "That man is not at all suitable! And to think that Allerton thought that I was lacking in gentility and the like when I first came to England." She let out a long slow breath, clearly trying to keep control of her anger. "He is being quite ridiculous, and I will not permit him to be so."

"I think he will understand that Lord Tolliver is not

suitable," Georgiana said hopefully. "He appeared just as astonished as we both did."

"I should hope so," Lady Allerton said loudly, drawing one or two glances which she did not seem to either notice or care about. "Foolish man! First he suggests Lord Pembrokeshire, and next he brings this fellow to greet you?" She shook her head, finally reaching the other side of the ballroom, which was, it seemed just as far away from Lord Tolliver as they could get. "I will have to speak very firmly to Allerton about this matter," she finished. "He must do better."

"If you are speaking of me, then I could not agree with you more."

With a squeak, Georgiana spun around, only to see Mr. Lowell looking at her in a most sheepish manner.

"Oh, Mr. Lowell," Georgiana stammered, yet again taken by surprise by his sudden appearance. "Good evening." It was not at all the done thing to eavesdrop on someone's conversation and then remark upon it, but it seemed that even Lady Allerton did not mind. She beamed at Mr. Lowell and nudged Georgiana to introduce them.

"How very fortunate you are here this evening," Georgiana said quickly, wondering if she could escape any further conversation with the gentleman should she introduce her sister-in-law. He was awkward and certainly a little out of place, but she did not want either her sister-in-law nor her brother to think there was anything at all between herself and Mr. Lowell, especially when her brother would think very poorly of such an acquaintance. "This is Lady Allerton, married to my brother last Season." A small smile captured Georgiana's lips as she saw just how eagerly Alice stepped forward. It must be wonderful to speak to someone who knew exactly what it felt like to be in another country and to find everything so very different from their own.

"I am very glad to meet you," Lady Allerton said as Mr. Lowell's face broke into a smile. "I hear you are from America. Might I ask where?"

"Boston," Mr. Lowell answered. "I came to visit my cousin, Lady Rutledge."

"I know the name, but have never been acquainted with her," Lady Allerton answered, apologetically. "I was only married last Season and have not spent much time in London as yet."

Mr. Lowell's expression remained bright. "Then I shall have to introduce you to her," he said with a small inclination of his head. "That is, after all, the correct way to go about things." With a wink, he leaned towards Georgiana, who felt a thrill race up her spine, sending a shiver straight through her. "I made a few mistakes the time we met, Lady Georgiana, and I must apologize for that." The smile faded, and a glimmer of frustration caught his eyes. "There is a good deal for me to learn."

"If you are speaking of the books you sent me, then there is nothing you need to apologize for," Georgiana answered, a little untruthfully. "It was very kind of you to do so."

"It was by way of thanks," he replied as she nodded and smiled graciously. "It has been difficult being here in London and finding things so different from home. I was very glad of your willingness to talk to me and to look past my mistakes. I believe I should have found someone who knew me *and* had a prior acquaintance with you before attempting to make any conversation."

The eager expression on his face and the warmth in his eyes made the last of Georgiana's reserve fall away. There was no need for her to further her acquaintance with Mr. Lowell, but it appeared that everything he had done, he had done entirely by mistake, and it was all entirely well-meant. He was an amiable gentleman, she decided, and she was glad that Lady Allerton had managed to make his acquaintance, for Georgiana was sure it would be good for them both.

"I can tell you of the many, *many* times I have made a mistake amongst the *ton*," Lady Allerton said with a wince. "Lord Allerton did not want to correct me at first and so chose instead to keep his distance—but we found a way through our difficulties in the end." She laughed at Mr. Lowell's almost mournful expression. "And you shall do so too. I am quite sure."

He shook his head, looking a little abashed. "I must hope so," he said, turning his gaze back to Georgiana and looking at her with such curiosity in his eyes, she felt her stomach tighten unexpectedly. "I believe, Lady Georgiana, that I must be introduced to your brother before I am allowed to ask if you can dance with me this evening."

Her breath caught, but she could not explain why. Was it because she did *not* want to dance with him, did not want the *ton* to be watching her as he led her around the floor?

"Oh, tosh!" Lady Allerton exclaimed, using a phrase that Georgiana knew came from her brother. "You need not worry, Mr. Lowell. You have become acquainted with me, and that, I am sure, will suffice. Please." She gestured towards Georgiana, who, given she could not now refuse nor shoot her sister-in-law a sharp look, had no other recourse but to look up at Mr. Lowell as he bowed his head, clearly trying his best to get everything just so.

"That is very kind of you, Lady Allerton, but I would prefer to—"

"Please," Georgiana interrupted, wanting Mr. Lowell to feel quite at his ease. "I would be glad to accept your invitation." She held out her dance card, looking at him with a warm smile. Mr. Lowell hesitated for a moment, then reached for it, looking at each of the dances with an inscrutable expression.

Georgiana's heart quickened as Mr. Lowell glanced up at her, a slightly wry smile on his face.

"I think I may very well embarrass you if I am not careful to choose a dance that I know very well indeed," he said awkwardly. "The country dance I am not familiar with, but the cotillion I believe I know very well."

She nodded, thinking the cotillion would be quite suitable. "Then the cotillion would suit me very well, Mr. Lowell." It would also mean she might garner a little less scrutiny than if he had chosen the waltz, which was, to her, something of a relief. "I thank you."

Mr. Lowell bit his lip, wrote his name down on the card, and then let the card slip from his fingers, so it dangled from her wrist again.

"I look forward to our dances, Lady Georgiana," he said, giving her a small bow and then turning his smile to Lady Allerton. "Lady Allerton, I hope that we will be able to talk at length another time. There is a lot more I'd like to ask."

"And it can be difficult to converse properly when one is surrounded by conversation and music," Lady Allerton agreed, making Mr. Lowell smile. "You must visit, you and your cousin, if you wish it."

"Then might I make the introductions?" Mr. Lowell asked, gesturing to his left and putting out his arm towards Lady Allerton. "That is the correct thing to do, isn't it?"

Lady Allerton laughed and accepted his arm, making Mr. Lowell's smile grow all the more. "It is," she told him, throwing a quick glance back towards Georgiana. "I would be very glad to be introduced to your cousin, Mr. Lowell."

Georgiana watched as Mr. Lowell and her sister-in-law stepped out together, allowing them to move away from her before she looked down at her dance card. There had been something very strange indeed about Mr. Lowell's remarks, for he had not said he was looking forward to their dance, but rather to their dances, which implied he had written his name down for more than one.

Her breath caught in her chest as she saw his name written for not one but two dances, with the second being the waltz. The waltz was the one she had hoped to avoid with him, for fear that being seen dancing in his arms would bring more questions and a flood of interest from the *beau monde*. What would her brother say?

Shaking her head to herself, Georgiana lifted her chin and tried to set her resolve. She would have to remove herself from the room during the waltz, perhaps stepping out into the gardens with Lady Allerton for a time. Or finding a quiet alcove where she might enjoy a refreshing glass of champagne. It might appear a little rude, but it would be better than having to step out onto the floor with him. He was not at all suitable for her and Georgiana knew very well that her brother would not take kindly to seeing her dancing the most intimate of dances with Mr. Lowell! Lady Allerton might not think there was much to it, but then again, she was still learning the ways of the *ton* and all the expectations that came with it.

Sighing to herself, Georgiana moved quickly away from Mr. Lowell and Lady Allerton, choosing to make her way back across the ballroom to find her brother and praying the intolerable Lord Tolliver was no longer present. It was obvious to them all, she hoped, that Lord Tolliver was not at all suitable and that, just as it had been with Lord Pembrokeshire, she could not possibly consider marriage to someone so unsuitable. She had to pray that her brother's considerations would improve, or that a gentleman within the *ton* would step forward and, for the first time in her life, ask if he might court her. Her heart warmed with that same familiar sense of longing, but Georgiana dashed it away. It had not occurred as yet, and she was not about to hope it would happen now just because she was back in London. Her brother's reputation and the awareness that he had been forced to marry a rich lady from America was still well known throughout the *beau monde,* and they did not forget easily, whether or not the marriage had become one of affection rather than requirement.

"Where is Lady Allerton?"

Georgiana looked up at her brother, taking in his heightened color. "She is speaking to Mr. Lowell," she said quietly, putting one hand on her brother's arm and seeing how he barely glanced at her. "There is nothing to concern yourself with, brother."

Lord Allerton closed his eyes and blew out his breath in evident frustration. "Is she still very angry with me?"

Georgiana hid a smile. "I fear she may well be," she answered, honestly, "but she is glad to have met Mr. Lowell and that, I think, will lift her spirits for a while."

"In that case, I suppose I should be grateful to this Mr. Lowell," Lord Allerton muttered, finally looking down at Georgiana. "He is the American, yes? The one who sent you *three* books?"

Again, Georgiana kept her smile hidden away. "Yes, that is he," she answered honestly. "But that was a mistake, brother. You know very well how difficult it was for Lady Allerton when she first arrived in London. Do not hold anything against Mr. Lowell."

"I will not," Lord Allerton answered firmly, his eyes determined. "Just so long as you are aware whilst such a match was suitable for me, it is not so for you."

Georgiana sighed inwardly, wishing that her brother would not immediately think she was drawn to Mr. Lowell. "I am well aware you married to Alice for her wealth and came from a situation where the ladies of the *ton* would not even look at you when it came to their daughters," she said pointedly as her brother dropped his head in embarrassment. "I am well aware I am expected to marry a well-titled gentleman of England, and I am more than contented to do so." She looked fixedly at her brother and prayed he would stop harping on about Mr. Lowell. "I am waiting, however, for you to find someone suitable rather than bringing gentlemen to me that are so entirely without merit."

Lord Allerton sighed heavily. "That is quite understandable," he admitted, spreading his hands. "Lady Allerton will help me also, I am sure."

"I must hope so," Georgiana muttered with a wryness in her eyes that her brother did not see, given his gaze turned back towards his wife.

"I should introduce myself to Mr. Lowell," Lord Allerton finished, with a long breath. "Unless...oh!"

Georgiana blinked in surprise, turning to see what it was that had caught her brother's attention, only to see Mr. Lowell coming towards her, his gaze fixed upon her. Her heart began to quicken, a flush of embarrassment climbing up her neck and into her cheeks as she saw the way other guests turned to look at him. He was not very well known in the *ton* as yet, and thus, they would be interested in knowing who he was.

"Lady Georgiana." Mr. Lowell bowed deeply in front of her as Georgiana bobbed a quick curtsy. "I believe this is our first dance of the evening." He extended a hand, a hopeful look in his eyes. "Shall we?"

Georgiana resisted the urge to pull up her dance card to look at it, realizing with horror that this was the waltz, the waltz she had intended to hide from. Having not realized it was to come upon her so quickly, she had made no attempt to move to the corner of the ballroom or to step outside and now was forced to accept his hand and to allow him to lead her out onto the floor. She avoided her brother's gaze as she walked beside Mr. Lowell, her face burning as she saw one or two people glancing at her and then turning to whisper to someone beside them.

"You don't think I will step on your toes, I hope?" Mr. Lowell asked with a broad smile as the first few notes began to play. "I know how to waltz, Lady Georgiana. I can waltz very well indeed."

Her smile was fixed as she stepped into his arms, looking pointedly over his shoulder rather than up into his face. "I can assure you that I have no such fears," she answered as he chuckled quietly. "Although you would not be the first gentleman to do so!"

He said nothing more but began to sweep her around the room, his grip firm and his steps sure. The tension that Georgiana had initially felt began to fade away, as did her fears as to what the *beau monde* might now be saying of her. Her hand loosened on Mr. Lowell's shoulder, thinking to herself he had told the truth when he had said he knew how to waltz and she had no concerns whatsoever he might trip nor stamp on her toes or any such thing. He was an excellent dancer, and Georgiana found herself relaxing into the dance and allowing herself to enjoy it.

"I thank you, Mr. Lowell," she murmured as the orchestra brought the waltz to a close. "You dance very well indeed."

"Perhaps it will make up for the rest of my flaws in the eyes of English society," he said, a wry smile twisting his mouth as he bowed. "Thank you for being willing to step out onto the floor with me, Lady Georgiana. I enjoyed it very much indeed."

"As did I," Georgiana answered as he led her from the floor, surprised to realize she truly meant it. She *had* enjoyed her waltz with Mr. Lowell and had found him to be an excellent dancer. Should he ask her again, at another ball, then she would have very little hesitation in accepting. "I enjoyed it very much, Mr. Lowell." Her eyes caught his, and she smiled at him. "Thank you."

CHAPTER FOUR

*T*he following afternoon found Oliver sitting quietly by the fire, reading a letter from his father that had arrived earlier that day. It spoke of how well things were going in Oliver's absence, which Oliver was grateful for even if it sent a surge of homesickness into his heart. He had taken over the finance business from his father some years ago, looking at the investments that were being made and ensuring he got the very best returns and, in the last few years, it had grown and grown all the more steadily, making him and his father very wealthy indeed. It was reassuring to know it was all going well in his absence, but there was a part of him that longed to return to all he knew. The ball last evening had been another example of his lack of understanding when it came to propriety and expectation, for he had made a few mistakes and had caught Lady Rutledge's embarrassed look on more than one occasion.

Although he *had* managed to dance with Lady Georgiana on two occasions and, after their waltz, had then been able to sign the dance cards of three other young ladies. One had been the daughter of a baron, with the second being the niece of a Viscount and the third dancing with him for the sake of Lady Rutledge, who was her close acquaintance. Oliver had been grateful for each person he had danced with, but he had not enjoyed any so much as he had done with Lady Georgiana. There had been a stiffness in her frame when they had first stepped out together, but within a minute or so, it had gone from her completely. She had relaxed into the dance and had swung around the floor with him without any hesitation, her steps firm and sure. He had enjoyed holding her in his arms immensely, finding his heart already a little affected by her presence and her company.

It was quite foolish of him to think of her in such a way, of course, so Oliver was doing all he could to set such feelings aside, telling himself he only enjoyed Lady Georgiana's company because of her kind nature and gentle spirit that had been so evident from the very first time they had met.

"Lowell?"

He looked up from his letter just in time, seeing Lady Rutledge practically throwing herself into the room, her cheeks flushed, her eyes bright with worry, and her skirts held up in one hand so she might scurry all the faster.

"Goodness, cousin!" he exclaimed, looking at her harassed expression. "Whatever is the matter?"

She shook her head, trying to catch her breath. "My dear Lowell, I must ask you a favor."

"Of course." He folded up the letter at once and

pushed it into his breast pocket. "What is it I can do for you, my dear cousin?"

Lady Rutledge came a little more into the room and flopped into a chair, her eyes still holding evidence of distress. "Might you go into town for me?"

"But of course."

She waved a hand. "I was to look over a new hat for Lord Rutledge—as a gift, you see—as well as some new gloves for him, but whilst they are ready for me to peruse, I have only just received a note from Lady Weatherly stating she will call upon me this afternoon. The dress-maker is expecting me, however, and given Lord Rutledge's gifts were to be given to him this evening, should all be as I expect, I find myself to be quite stuck in difficulty!"

Oliver smiled at his cousin. "Why don't you just tell this Lady Weatherly you cannot meet with her?"

Lady Rutledge looked quite horrified. "She is the wife of a Marquess!" she exclaimed as understanding washed over Oliver. "A marchioness cannot be refused anything."

"Of course not," Oliver agreed quietly. "And the hat and gloves are to be given to Lord Rutledge this evening, you say?"

"In time for the ball tomorrow," Lady Rutledge answered, reminding Oliver that Lord and Lady Rutledge were themselves throwing a ball tomorrow evening—a ball he was very much looking forward to. "It was to be a gift, you see, and I would very much like to give it to him still, if I can."

Oliver rose from his chair without waiting another

moment. "I quite understand," he said, coming across to his cousin and reaching down to pat her hand. "Enjoy your visit with Lady Weatherly, my dear. I shall make sure the hat and gloves are well made and to the highest standard and will bring them back here for you."

Lady Rutledge seemed to collapse back just a little in her chair. "I thank you," she breathed, clearly no longer alarmed. "You are very kind, Lowell."

He chuckled. "Not at all," he answered with a rueful smile. "After all the trouble I have given you thus far, this is the very least that I can do."

"You do not bring trouble," she corrected with a sharp look up towards him, her eyes bright. "You did very well last evening, Lowell. I was very glad to see you dancing so well, and I am sure the *ton* thought well of it also."

Knowing the view and considerations of the *ton* ought to be of great importance to him, Oliver tried to smile even though he felt the weight of the *beau monde's* condescension whenever he set foot outside the house. "That is very good of you to say, cousin," he answered without saying whether or not he agreed with her. "Now, I should go before I make the mistake of accidentally meeting Lady Weatherly in the hallway and saying something that is either deemed inappropriate or a little lacking in manners." He grinned at Lady Rutledge, who shooed him away with a teasing look in her eyes, telling him the name of the dressmakers just as he closed the door tightly behind him.

~

"They look very well made indeed." Oliver glanced up at the dressmaker, whose cheeks had colored a little red as he smiled at her. "I am sure Lady Rutledge will be very pleased indeed."

"I shall have them wrapped for you directly," the dressmaker answered, closing the box and leaving it on the counter for a moment. "And now, the hat." She picked up a large box from the floor and lifted it to the counter, opening it up to reveal a top hat that would befit any gentleman of the *ton*. He looked at it carefully, picking it up and allowing his well-trained eyes to run over each seam. It was without fault or flaw, he realized, thinking silently to himself that his cousin had picked an excellent dressmaker.

"That is perfect," he murmured, looking at the dressmaker who flushed a deep scarlet but bobbed a quick curtsy. "So well made, in fact, that I would like to purchase one also." He hesitated, then smiled. "And some new gloves and a new coat too."

The dressmaker blinked for a moment or two, then began to smile. "I would be glad to assist you, sir," she said looking him up and down as if assessing his frame. "Would you like to have one specifically made for you?"

Oliver went into the finer details of his new coat for a few minutes, arranging everything quickly and then asking the dressmaker to ensure the bill was written out for him at once, as he would like to pay for it all this afternoon. The dressmaker nodded and hurried away, leaving Oliver to meander around the shop, looking at various things and finding himself in a happier state of mind than he had been when reading his father's letter.

The *ton* would slowly begin to accept him, he was sure. Having met with Lady Allerton last evening, he knew that if *she* had been welcomed by the *beau monde,* then there was every chance he would be too, once he stopped making foolish mistakes like introducing himself to young ladies whom he did not know!

"Oh, excuse me!"

Having had his gaze caught on what was a bright red ribbon, Oliver stumbled back, realizing he had walked into someone. "I am so very sorry," he said at once, his cheeks flaming with color as he looked at the lady, who was brushing down her gown as if he had somehow creased it. "I didn't mean to—I mean, I should have been watching where I was going."

The lady looked up at him, her eyes as blue as the sea and her skin as white as the flakes of snow that had only just begun to fall outside. Her gaze was considering but not angry, her thin lips twisted as she studied him, perhaps wondering whether or not she ought to rail at him. She was no debutante, of that, he was sure, but there was still a youthfulness to her that had Oliver wondering where her chaperone might be.

"Forgive me," he said inclining his head again. "I did not see you, but that was entirely my fault."

"Yes," the lady said, her tone firm as her voice rang out across the room. "Yes, it was your fault, sir."

Heat climbed up Oliver's spine, but he did not look away. It had been his fault, his doing, his mistake—and just when he had been telling himself not to make any more missteps!

"I was distracted by one of the many lovely items in

this shop," he said as though this explanation would bring him any sympathy. "I should have been much more careful."

The lady tipped her head to the left, still watching him with that cool, firm gaze. "What was it, sir?"

He frowned. "What do you mean?"

"What was it that caught your attention?" she asked, the tiniest of smiles catching the corner of her mouth and, as it did so, entirely transforming her features. "Was it something quite lovely?"

A little relieved she was not about to give him a resounding set-down, Oliver nodded and gestured to the ribbons on his right. "The colors are quite vivid," he said as though this were a clear enough explanation. "I thought to mayhap purchase one."

"Oh?" The lady's smile grew, her eyes now a little brighter than before. "For whom would you purchase such a lovely thing?" The interest in her gaze surprised him, as did the forwardness of her manner. He had been told that such profound interest in a stranger was not well thought of, and yet this lady here was doing the very thing he had been warned against.

"It is for my cousin," he said slowly, wondering what she meant by such a question and why she still did not have any chaperone. "That is all."

The lady's smile slipped for a moment. "I see," she said softly. "And when are you to marry?"

Oliver was overcome with astonishment, staring at the lady with wide eyes. He had never expected such a question and certainly not from someone who was a veritable stranger! It was entirely improper, of that, he was quite sure, and yet she had asked him without even a momentary hesitation.

"Is the wedding to be before Christmas or after?" the lady asked again when he did not immediately answer. "And is it to be here in London?"

"I—I am not to marry," he answered, stammering just a little with the astonishment that came from her question. "I have no intention of doing so."

"Oh." Her smile grew again. "I thought you were a gentleman from a far off land come to lay claim to your cousin's hand!"

At this remark, Oliver could not help but smile. "I fear I am nothing so mysterious, my lady," he answered, inclining his head just a fraction. "My cousin is Lady Rutledge, and it is for her that I would purchase this ribbon."

"How very thoughtful of you!" the lady cried, one hand over her heart. "I am acquainted with Lady Rutledge, of course." Her eyes lingered on his, igniting a sense of awkwardness in his heart at the intensity of her gaze. "I have been very ill-mannered, have I not?" she asked teasingly and showing no sign of changing her manner despite her obvious awareness she was being so. "But I am afraid that with being a widow, one needs to gain a little more boldness than before." Her eyes twinkled. "I am no shy, retiring debutante, sir, as you can see."

"Indeed," he agreed, hoping he was not insulting her by stating such a thing. "Might I ask your name?"

She laughed, the sound filling the shop. "Of course you may!" she smiled, her eyes dancing. "It is quite improper to be making such introductions this way, but given how we have met, we shall have to hope it will suffice." She bobbed a quick curtsy, her smile never fading. "I am Lady Northcott."

"And I am Mr. Lowell," he answered, seeing the interest flickering in her eyes. "I come from Boston."

"And what do you do, Mr. Lowell from Boston?"

Her sing-song voice made him wince inwardly, feeling an awkward tension he could not quite shake. "I have recently taken over my father's financial business," he said with a small smile. "I am only here to visit my cousin and shall soon return."

Lady Northcott looked immediately dismayed. "But not too soon, I hope?" she said, taking a small step forward. "We have only just become acquainted, and I confess that I am quite intrigued by you. A gentleman from another part of the world, which I know very little about." Her expression became all the more troubled. "My late husband used to go to the continent *very* often so as to secure his interests there, but he never once went to America."

Oliver smiled politely, feeling very confused as to this lady's conduct and manner of speaking. She was being very open with him when he had been told to keep such remarks until an acquaintance was more firmly established. Perhaps, he considered, being a widow meant the lady could be a little more unorthodox and would not be looked down on because of it.

"I hope to return after Christmas," he said with a small shrug. "I could depart at any time, but given what I have been told of Christmas here in England, I think I should like to remain and see for myself what it is like."

"Oh, yes, you must indeed!" the lady declared, her smile returning to her face almost at once. "And you must come to the soiree I am to have in a few days' time. It will be quite lovely to be able to introduce you to some of my acquaintances. I am sure they will be just as intrigued with you as I."

Oliver, a little confused still but feeling also quite flattered at the lady's warmth, found himself nodding. "I would be delighted to attend," he said honestly. "Thank you."

The door to the shop opened, and the affixed bell tinkled as it was pushed open wide. Two ladies hurried in, one of them exclaiming furiously about the weather and the snow, whilst the second brushed down her arms, letting the snowflakes fall to the floor.

Oliver, a little surprised, looked out of the shop window, astonished to see what appeared to be sheets of white falling to the ground, one after the other. It had been falling for some time, it appeared, but he had not noticed given his conversation with first the dressmaker and then with Lady Northcott. "Goodness!" he exclaimed, moving towards the window to look out at the scene a little more. "I didn't expect the snow to be this heavy here in London!"

Lady Northcott joined him and laughed. "Indeed! It can be very cold here. Did you know that we have the Frost Fair every year, held out on the ice?"

He turned to stare at her, his eyes wide with astonishment. "Really?"

"Indeed we do," came another voice, as Oliver turned to see none other than Lady Georgiana standing there, accompanied by her sister-in-law. "The Frost Fair is a remarkable affair, and I would encourage you to see it when the time comes." She smiled, although Oliver thought her expression a little tight as she bobbed a quick curtsy to Lady Northcott. "Good afternoon, Lady Northcott."

"Good afternoon," Lady Northcott replied a touch coolly. "And good afternoon to you also, Lady Allerton."

"Good afternoon." Lady Allerton was not smiling, her gaze almost cold as she looked steadily back at Lady Northcott. "You have met Mr. Lowell, it seems."

Oliver cleared his throat, feeling a sense of awkwardness. "Yes, we have just introduced ourselves," he said wincing inwardly as he saw Lady Georgiana frown. Evidently, she must think him just as foolish as before. "Given the weather, it seemed a little rude to be standing in the same shop without a single word of introduction!"

This, it seemed, brought a little relief to Lady Georgiana, for her expression lightened a touch as she glanced from himself to Lady Northcott and back again. Lady Allerton, however, remained unsmiling.

"You also *must* come to my little soiree, Lady Allerton," Lady Northcott cooed, moving a little closer to Oliver as though she were very well acquainted with him. "I have just had Mr. Lowell's agreement he will attend, and I am sure that, since you are acquainted with him, he would very much appreciate it if you were to be there also." She smiled warmly up at him, her beautiful face filled with nothing but kindness, although Oliver could not help but feel a little uncomfortable when she put one hand on his arm.

Lady Georgiana sent a look to Lady Allerton that Oliver could not quite decipher. It was as if she did not want to accept the invitation but felt obliged to, given what Lady Northcott had said about Oliver's eagerness to have some acquaintances present. He wanted to say there was no need for them to come, no need for them to feel as though he would be lost without them present, but found that every time he came to say something, his mouth refused to move.

"That is very kind of you, Lady Northcott," Lady Allerton said eventually, clearly a trifle reluctant. "We would be very glad to accept."

"Wonderful!" Lady Northcott clapped her hands in evident delight, then stepped away from Oliver, gesturing towards the window. "And I can see the snow is lessening, so I must take my leave before it worsens again. I shall send you all an invitation directly."

"Thank you, Lady Northcott," Oliver called after her, seeing how she threw him a dazzling smile. "I look forward to your little gathering."

She waved a hand delicately, then stepped outside and disappeared into the snow, leaving Oliver standing opposite Lady Allerton and Lady Georgiana, who were both looking at him with similar expressions of scrutiny.

"It looks very cold outside," Oliver said by way of finding something to say instead of allowing the awkward silence to continue. "Did you find it difficult coming through the snow?"

Lady Georgiana cleared her throat gently, but instead of breaking the tension, the sound only added to it. "We had no particular difficulty," she said, no sense of warmth in her voice but rather that reserve he had seen ever since she had entered the shop. "But it may take a little longer to return home."

"Mr. Lowell?"

The dressmaker was back at the counter, a piece of paper in her hand. Excusing himself and grateful for the distraction, Oliver hurried back towards her, pasting a smile on his face he did not quite feel.

"Your bill, sir," the dressmaker said. "And your items are ready to take back to Lady Rutledge."

"Thank you." Quickly, he paid his bill in full and listened as the dressmaker told him when his coat, hat, and gloves would be ready for him. Thanking her again, he turned back to take his leave of Lady Georgiana and Lady Allerton, seeing how they were speaking quietly together, their heads close so he could not overhear them.

"I should take these things back to Lady Rutledge," he said with a small shrug. "And the weather does look very poor. I do hope you will get home safely."

"I am sure we will," Lady Allerton answered, her eyes still holding more emotion than she was expressing. "We will see you tomorrow evening, I hope? At Lord and Lady Rutledge's ball."

He nodded. "Yes, of course." A little emboldened, he looked towards Lady Georgiana, who appeared to be chewing her lip. "And I hope you will dance with me again, Lady Georgiana."

She pressed her lips together, not giving him an immediate answer. A second or two of silence passed before she nodded and looked away, leaving him only with that particular answer rather than anything of significance.

"Wonderful," he said a trifle doubtfully. "Until tomorrow, then."

"Until tomorrow," Lady Allerton replied, leaving Oliver wondering what it was he had done that had caused such a change in both their manners and fearing that, yet again, Lady Rutledge would have yet more to discuss with him before tomorrow evening's ball had even begun.

CHAPTER FIVE

"I have found you the perfect match."

Georgiana looked doubtfully at her brother, seeing how he sat back in the carriage with a look of immense pride on his face.

"Oh?" she queried, looking at her sister-in-law, who was, to her surprise, looking quite contented with this news. The carriage came to a stop just outside Lord Rutledge's home, and within a few moments, the door was pulled open by the waiting footmen.

Lord Allerton gestured for both Georgiana and Lady Allerton to exit the carriage before him, forcing Georgiana to wait until he had joined them on the cold, wintry street. "Who is it this time, Allerton?" Georgiana asked, growing both a little impatient and a little anxious. "I hope it is not someone similar in any way to Lord Tolliver or Lord Pembrokeshire!"

Lord Allerton chuckled, offering his arm to Lady Allerton before climbing the few steps towards the front door. "No, indeed not," he said heartily. "It is, in fact, the Earl of Poole."

Georgiana hesitated, searching her memory to see if she knew the gentleman. "I do not think I know him, Allerton," she said as she stepped through the front door and immediately joined the receiving line. "Might I ask how you are acquainted with him?" She dropped her voice low, not wanting any of the other guests to overhear her. "Is he well known to you?"

"He is," her brother said cheerfully. "I have known him for a long time. In fact, he has never come to London for the Season—either in the summer or in the little Season, but this time he has decided to attend."

Georgiana swallowed hard, feeling a sudden lump in her throat, although she could not quite explain why. She had known this was coming, had known that her brother would be finding someone for her to marry, and yet now he had done so, now he seemed to be quite certain that this particular gentleman would be suitable for her, Georgiana felt terrified. Had she still had the hope that someone would come along who was, in fact, interested in her simply because of their prior acquaintance?

"He has decided he now needs to marry and, given he has dragged himself to London in order to do such a thing, I thought I might suggest an agreement."

"I see," Georgiana murmured, her throat still very dry, and her hands tightly clenched as she moved towards Lord and Lady Rutledge, ready to greet them and thank them for their invitation.

"Therefore, whilst the particulars still have to be worked out, a marriage between yourself and Lord Poole will occur. Perhaps after Christmas, given we only have less than three weeks until then."

Georgiana nodded but was unable to say more, being forced to turn and greet her hosts, finally looking towards the ballroom and feeling her heart lift at the sight of it.

"Thank you for inviting me," she said as she curtsied in front of Lord and Lady Rutledge. "The ballroom looks quite wonderful!"

"I do so love Christmastime," Lady Rutledge answered with a sigh of contentment. "It has been lovely to oversee the decoration of the ballroom, I confess. I do hope you enjoy this evening." She smiled at Georgiana, who smiled back and then turned to make her way into the room itself.

The ballroom was truly splendid. Strands of ivy and holly berries were twined together into wreaths, which hung around the room at various points, and she spied two boughs of mistletoe, each hung on either side of the room. A faint blush caught her cheeks as she looked at them, wondering if she would have any gentlemen seeking to steal a kiss from her in exchange for a mistletoe berry. Gold and silver ribbons caught her attention, the warm crackling fire spreading orange and red lights all across the room. A footman cleared his throat gently, holding out a tray towards her, and Georgiana took a glass at once. She lifted it to her lips and took a sip, a smile spreading across her face at the delicious syllabub. Lady Rutledge had truly outdone herself.

"Should you like me to introduce him to you this evening?"

She started, looking to see her brother coming to

stand beside her, with Lady Allerton next to him. For a moment, she had forgotten about what her brother had planned for her only for it all to come back to her in a rush, making her swallow hard.

"He is here this evening, then?"

Lord Allerton nodded. "He is," he said, looking through the crowd as though he might spot him immediately. "Or he should be. I would like to introduce him to you, Georgiana. Even Alice agrees he is a suitable match."

"I do," Lady Allerton confirmed with a small smile. "I have met him only once, but I think him a good match for you, Georgiana."

Georgiana took a little comfort from this, knowing that her sister-in-law would not consider accepting someone she thought was even a *little* unsuitable for her. "Then I should be glad to meet him," she told her brother, who looked quite contented at this.

"Good!" he declared, putting a hand on Georgiana's shoulder. "I do want you to be happy and settled with a good husband and nothing to fear for the rest of your days, dear sister. I am sure Lord Poole will ensure you have a life of contentment."

Georgiana let her eyes lift to her brother's face and saw there the consideration and the care he had for her. It had not always been present in his life, had certainly been absent completely on some occasions, but at this moment, at this time, she was truly grateful for it. What was she to do? Was she to reject Lord Poole because she wanted to hold onto a faint hope that another gentleman might show her some genuine interest and therefore seek to court her? She knew the chance of such a thing happening was very small indeed, and her practical mind told her she ought not to be so foolish.

"Thank you, Allerton," she said quietly as her brother smiled. "You are very good to me, and I appreciate your consideration."

"It is the very least I can do after my foolish behavior," he told her, his hand lifting from her shoulder as he turned to look at Lady Allerton. "And you have Alice to thank for this also. Without her, I do not think I would have ever managed to find someone suitable for you, given how ridiculous my first two suggestions have been!"

"Then I thank you also, Alice," Georgiana said honestly. "And I look forward to meeting Lord Poole very soon."

~

"You are looking quite lovely this evening, Lady Georgiana."

Georgiana smiled at Mr. Lowell as he came towards her, seeing how he bowed carefully and then tucked his hands behind his back, holding himself tall as any gentleman might.

"I thank you for your very kind compliment, Mr. Lowell," she answered, aware she was still feeling very nervous about her meeting with Lord Poole and hoping the strain did not show in her manner. "And are you enjoying the ball this evening?"

He grinned. "I am," he said with a chuckle. "Everyone present wishes to speak well of my cousin so, despite the fact that I have no title and that I do not come from England, they are being more than polite to me. And that even with my many mistakes!"

"I am sure you are doing very well," Georgiana replied firmly. "Although..." She trailed off, biting her lip and remaining as uncertain as she had been yesterday as to whether or not she ought to say something about Lady Northcott, whom Mr. Lowell had been speaking to yesterday afternoon.

"Is there something you wish to say, Lady Georgiana?" Mr. Lowell asked with a slight look of concern. "Is it, in fact, to do with yesterday afternoon when we met in the shop?"

Georgiana's eyes flared wide, seeing the immediate reaction on Mr. Lowell's face as she tried to explain.

"I was very well aware both yourself and Lady Allerton were rather...cautious when it came to my new acquaintance," Mr. Lowell said with a slightly wry look. "I have not mentioned it to Lady Rutledge for fear she would rail at me again when she was already very busy indeed with the preparations for the ball, but I would appreciate it if you were honest with me about what I did wrong."

"Oh, no, no!" Georgiana exclaimed, putting one hand out towards him. "No, Mr. Lowell, you are not to think you have anything to concern yourself with as regards Lady Northcott." She shook her head, recalling how she and Lady Allerton had talked at length about what they should have done or if they had any right to say anything to Mr. Lowell at all. "I do not want you to think even for a moment that there is anything you have done you need to concern yourself with."

"Then it must be to do with Lady Northcott," he said with a frown. "I will be honest with you, Lady Georgiana, if I may—I found her very...unusual."

Georgiana blinked. "Unusual?" she repeated, tilting her head and looking at him carefully. "Might I ask in what way?"

Mr. Lowell hesitated. "I found her to be the opposite of what I have been told to expect," he said slowly. "I don't want to start speaking ill of her, given I know that would be rudeness itself—but I have been instructed very carefully not to introduce myself to a lady, to keep conversation somewhat bland until a better friendship is established, and never to appear overfamiliar."

"And Lady Northcott was all of those things," Georgiana finished for him, seeing him nod slowly. She sighed heavily, trying to choose her words with the greatest of care. "I will start by saying that I have no intention of speaking ill of Lady Northcott, which was why both myself and Lady Allerton struggled to know whether or not we should speak to you."

Mr. Lowell took a small step closer to her, his eyes fixed on hers—and Georgiana felt her stomach tighten.

"I would be more than a little grateful for any insight, Lady Georgiana," he said humbly. "If you haven't noticed already, I am driving Lady Rutledge near to madness with my constant failings."

"I hardly think that is true," Georgiana answered, seeing his rueful smile but feeling her heart ache for him. "I cannot imagine how difficult it must be for you. I have been brought up with it all, so I feel as though I have always known what is expected of me, whereas you..." Closing her eyes for a moment, she let out a long breath and then looked at him again. "Lady Northcott is a widow, Mr. Lowell. She has very specific intentions at the present moment." His eyes remained blank, and there was no clear understanding of what she was saying. All the more embarrassed, Georgiana closed her eyes and tried to think of what to say to help him understand. "She enjoys the friendship of certain gentlemen who might be willing to give her some financial assistance in exchange for her company." Unable to look at him straight in the face, Georgiana turned away just a little, aware of just how hot her face now had become. "Might I ask if she asked about your background?"

Mr. Lowell cleared his throat and, daring a glance at him, Georgiana saw he too was flushed. "She did, yes," he stated, his voice low and rather gruff. "I quite understand, Lady Georgiana. Thank you for telling me."

A sudden tense laugh escaped from Georgiana's mouth as Mr. Lowell's eyes shot back towards hers—and they were both laughing. The tension and awkwardness shattered at once, and Georgiana found Mr. Lowell's face transformed into a bright, warm expression, his eyes dancing as he shook his head.

"Goodness, Lady Georgiana, I don't think you know just how grateful I am to you," Mr. Lowell said once they had managed to regain their composure. "If I had told

Lady Rutledge what had happened with Lady Northcott, I do believe she would have sent me back to America almost at once!" Sighing heavily, he gave her a rueful smile. "I think I will need a good deal more guidance from you, Lady Georgiana."

Pulling out a handkerchief from her pocket, Georgiana dabbed at her eyes, relieved there was no awkwardness between them now. "I would be glad to help you in any way I can, Mr. Lowell," she found herself saying, a little surprised by her willingness. "I know that society is difficult enough to traverse as it is, and to have to come into it now and attempt to learn all that is required and expected in a short time must be almost impossible."

Mr. Lowell tilted his head to one side, studying her closely. "Would you truly be willing, Lady Georgiana?" he asked quietly. "My poor cousin is quite worn out with me, and I know she would be grateful for your input."

Georgiana found herself nodding, surprised at just how fervently she found herself wanting to help him. This was most unorthodox, of course, for she had no reason to assist him given he was not her relative nor even close friend, but something had shifted in her acquaintance with him, and Georgiana's heart was now filled with compassion for his struggles. "I know Lady Allerton would be very glad to continue her acquaintance with you," she said with a smile. "I will make sure you are given an invitation to dine with us very soon."

"And might I visit you one afternoon?" he asked, looking a little awkward. "That is permitted, I hope?"

Again, she laughed, seeing how confused he was.

"Yes, that is permitted," she said with a wave of her hand. "How long is it until you leave for America?"

He shrugged, looking at her thoughtfully. "I have not yet decided," he said with a shrug. "If I leave soon, I *might* make it back home in time for Christmas, but it is unlikely."

"Then you must wait until after Christmas has passed," she said lightly, feeling a strange sense of happiness he was willing to stay in England a little longer. "Experience Christmas as it is here, for when are you going to have such an opportunity again?"

He nodded, his expression still thoughtful. "That is a wise suggestion," he agreed, making her blush just a little. "Thank you, Lady Georgiana. Might I visit you tomorrow?"

"That would be a good idea, I think," she agreed, with a wry smile. "Lady Northcott's soiree is in two days' time, so mayhap we should discuss what you absolutely must not do, regardless of how Lady Northcott presses you." She arched one eyebrow, and Mr. Lowell chuckled, shaking his head again.

"I think that would be an excellent idea," he agreed, a little ruefully. "Now, a dance, perhaps? And then I should let you return to your brother. He appears to be searching for you."

Georgiana turned her head and saw her brother only a short distance away, looking meaningfully at her. Her stomach dropped, and she swallowed hard, very anxious.

"Yes, a dance. Of course." Holding out her dance card, Georgiana did not even notice where Mr. Lowell wrote his name, her smile disappearing as the knowledge of who she was to meet next hit her.

"Thank you, Lady Georgiana," Mr. Lowell said, bowing with a flourish. "You are truly a very kind and considerate lady, and I am very glad to have made your acquaintance."

A tiny smile caught the corner of her mouth. "Very proper, Mr. Lowell," she said curtsying. "And if you would excuse me now, I must go and speak to my brother."

"Good evening, Lord Poole."

Georgiana held her breath as a fair-haired gentleman turned around from where he had been speaking to someone else, looking at Lord Allerton and grunting in a gruff manner. She glanced at the person moving away from him, a little surprised to note it was none other than Lady Northcott. Her attention was soon swiftly drawn back to Lord Poole's face as her brother beamed in her direction, clearly delighted at this meeting.

"I thought to present my sister to you," Lord Allerton continued as Georgiana forced herself to look directly into Lord Poole's face. She saw a broad-shouldered gentleman with a square jaw and sharp green eyes that were fixed upon her own. He was not unhandsome, with his long roman nose and thick, fair hair that was swept neatly to one side. However, there was no light in his eyes, no smile on his lips, and a coldness about his manner that made Georgiana want to shiver.

"Lady Georgiana." Lord Poole bowed slowly, a little stiffly. "How very good to meet you this evening."

"Lord Poole," she replied, curtsying beautifully and lifting her chin to look back into his eyes, telling herself not to allow her first impression to push her away from him. Both her brother and Lady Allerton thought that Lord Poole was a good match. Therefore, she expected him to have a decent character, which she certainly could not expect to see within the first few minutes of their meeting! "I am glad to make your acquaintance." She placed a light smile on her lips and waited for him to speak, expecting him to make some conversation, but as the seconds ticked by, Georgiana began to realize he had no intention of saying anything more. Finding this to be very awkward indeed, she looked to her brother, only to discover that Lord Allerton had melted away and was now standing a few steps to Lord Poole's left, talking animatedly with another acquaintance, evidently still able to see Georgiana from where he stood.

"Are you enjoying this evening?" she asked, her voice a little higher pitched with the strain of trying to make conversation with someone who did not appear to be interested in speaking to her. "My brother says you have not often been in London."

"There has been no need to be present before," he told her with a small sniff as his eyes drifted across the crowd. "And once the agreement between myself and your brother is finalized, there will be no need for me to remain."

Georgiana had to force herself to remain standing calmly in front of Lord Poole when everything in her wanted to exclaim aloud. Why would a newly betrothed gentleman return to his estate when there would be so much to prepare? Did he not want to spend time with her, so they might get to know each other a little better?

"I have a townhouse here, of course," Lord Poole continued as if this was something of particular interest. "My brother also resides in London, but his townhouse is in a part of London I have no inclination towards visiting." Again, he sniffed as though such a thought brought him a sense of disgust. Georgiana felt her skin crawl. This gentleman clearly had no consideration for anyone but himself.

"I look forward to returning to my estate," Lord Poole finished dryly, his eyes running over the assembled crowd as though he were much higher above them, much better in status than they. "Thankfully, I will not have to linger unless the snow should prevent my travel." This was said with a deep, angry frown that made it appear as though Lord Poole would be disgruntled with nature itself, seeing it as something preventing him from achieving what he wished.

"We will marry in the parish at my brother's estate, surely," she said slowly, watching him carefully but seeing no reaction on his almost expressionless face. "That will mean you will have to travel from your estate to his. Surely it would be better to remain here in London so that we might spend time in each other's company."

His eyes appeared to be a little glazed as he sighed and looked at her discontentedly. "There is no need for such things," he said quite calmly. "You know your expectations as my wife, and I know my expectations as your husband. Therefore, we should rub along well enough together, I am sure."

Georgiana did not know what to say to this. She had never thought the gentleman she would marry would be practically a stranger—a stranger who clearly had no intention of knowing her better! Was that all he wanted from her? A lady who would know her duty and fulfill it without question?

"Your dowry is sufficient, so I can see no need for any delay," Lord Poole finished with another sniff that began to irritate Georgiana intently. "I should be able to return to my estate within the next ten days or so, once we have decided the wedding date and, as you have said, the place we shall marry."

"And are we never to converse?" Georgiana asked, feeling a mixture of both upset and anger. "We are not to talk a walk together in the park, or even take tea?"

Lord Poole looked quite confused. "My dear lady, why should you even think of such things?" he asked in a tone that suggested she was being quite ridiculous. "We are to wed. There will be plenty of time to further our regard for each other in the years to follow." With a small wave of his hand, he thrust her questions even further away. "No, the practical arrangements will be seen to first. Thereafter, we might consider conversing and the like."

"But what if I do not suit?" she demanded, seeing how he attempted to step away and feeling riled all the more. "What if I am much too obnoxious for you? What if I do not have all the requirements you expect from a wife?" She threw up her hands, her eyes fixed on his. "I do not play the pianoforte particularly well, for example."

Lord Poole leaned in, his green eyes darkening. "But you do play the harp exceedingly well," he said softly. "Have no fear, Lady Georgiana, I have spoken to your brother at length and know you very well indeed."

She gave a slight shudder, looking up into his green eyes and seeing them as cold as emeralds, glittering in an almost ominous fashion. This gentleman would care nothing for her. He spoke of there being regard growing between them in the years that would follow, but Georgiana could already tell there would be no such thing. This gentleman was not someone with a kind spirit, a gentle smile, and a warmth in his eyes. He was cold and calculating, seeing this marriage as nothing more than a solution to his requirement for marriage. She would be used to produce the heir, perhaps an additional child thereafter, and nothing more. Her hope for a life of contentment and happiness seemed likely to remain unfulfilled.

And yet, there was nothing she could say to refuse Lord Poole. He was, as her brother and sister-in-law had decided, quite suitable. He had a title, a good fortune, and would be able to keep her in comfort for the rest of her days. His manner was stiff and formal but not rude or arrogant, as Lord Tolliver had been. All that was lacking was any sense he might truly come to care for her. Georgiana was certain Lord Poole would keep her at arm's length for the rest of her life, confining her to a world of loneliness.

Her mind filled with the memory of Mr. Lowell and

how they had shared laughter and understanding only a few minutes before. Why she was thinking of him, she could not say, but in her heart, Georgiana knew that what she had shared with Mr. Lowell was the kind of thing she longed to share with her future husband.

But it seemed that dream was not to be fulfilled. With Lord Poole to be her husband, there could never be that friendship she so longed for. She was trapped, it seemed, and there was nothing for her to do but accept that this was now her future.

CHAPTER SIX

"Good evening, Lady Northcott."

Oliver bowed low as Lady Northcott put out one hand towards him, her eyes twinkling up at him as he took it gently. He bowed over it as he knew was expected but did not allow his lips to touch her skin. That would give her the wrong impression, and it was something he distinctly wanted to avoid.

Knowing the lady's intentions as he now did, Oliver was doing all he could to ensure he behaved with absolute propriety. There was still that sense of awkwardness that had begun to come over him when he had first met the lady, although she seemed quite oblivious to it. Either that or she hoped that her warmth towards him would ensure he returned her friendly advances.

"I am so *very* glad you could attend," Lady Northcott said with a bright smile. "You will know a few guests here, of course, and Lady Allerton and Lady Georgiana have only just arrived." She gestured with one hand out towards the large drawing-room where a few guests milled around. There was an open door that must, Oliver thought, lead to another room where mayhap there was a pianoforte and the like, given Lady Northcott had said there would be music at some point in the evening.

"I will make sure to speak to you a little later," she continued as he took a step away from her. "But first, I must do my duties as hostess."

A little perturbed as to what Lady Northcott wanted to say to him, Oliver nodded, smiled, and walked a bit further into the room, his eyes searching all over for someone he already knew. The room itself was large and very well decorated, with touches of splendor here and there. Oliver wondered if they might sing some carols a little later in the evening, which was something he had not yet done since his arrival in England. Much to his surprise, Oliver found himself questioning whether or not Lady Georgiana could sing and if she enjoyed Christmas carols, with a vision of her throwing her head back and singing with the joy of the Season coming filling his mind. A frown marred his brow as he gave himself a slight shake. There was no need for him to be thinking of Lady Georgiana in that way. He was grateful to her for her willingness to offer him assistance as he traversed through society, but there was to be nothing more than that. He was to return to America soon and did not need to leave his heart behind him here in England.

Will you ever marry?

The thought struck him hard, his heart slamming against his chest as he stumbled slightly. He had never considered marriage, finding himself quite contented with life such as it was. In taking over his father's business, Oliver had been blessed with more money than he would ever require, and thus had considered nothing more than ensuring his financial interests remained sound. He supposed he would have to marry if he was to ensure there was someone to continue the business in his stead, but it was not something he needed to give much thought to at present.

At least, he didn't think he needed to.

"Mr. Lowell, you have made it at last!"

The teasing voice of Lady Allerton caught his attention, turning him around to look into her laughing face.

"I was a little late, yes," he admitted, somewhat ruefully. "Lady Georgiana was good enough to explain to me the nature of our hostess, and so I thought it might be best to be a little later than expected."

Lady Allerton shook her head, her eyes still bright. "I am sorry if I should have said something sooner," she replied with a small shrug. "It is one of these very difficult situations where one is never quite sure what is the right thing to do."

He smiled at her, studying her for a moment. "You have done very well, I think, Lady Allerton."

A slight frown caught her brow. "Done well?"

"In fitting in here," he said with a small sigh. "I am well aware I am treated with respect, but there is much about my manner that is wrong. Lady Rutledge was going almost crazy with the effort of trying to teach me."

Lady Allerton laughed ruefully, her eyes holding something that Oliver could not quite make out. Regret? Sorrow?

"I am sure you will manage to fit into society in the

end," she told him with a slight shrug. "Yes, it has been difficult at times, but I have succeeded—and that is without forcing myself to do and say all that was expected!" Another laugh escaped her at the astonished look on his face. "You look surprised, Mr. Lowell, but it is true! You can ask Lord Allerton if you wish since he will attest to it. I was quite determined not to become the perfect English lady, given I am neither English nor a lady!" Her eyes twinkled, her lips catching in what was a rueful smile. "There are standards, of course, and I have done my best to ensure I behave *correctly*, given I am now a Countess, but I will not have the snobbery, the arrogance, nor the expected love of gossip that comes with my title." Her expression grew a little hard as she glanced around the room. "To many here, I am still unfit to be a Countess, but that does not matter to me. My husband holds me in deep affection, as I do him, and that, Mr. Lowell, is all that matters to me."

Finding himself nodding, Oliver smiled at Lady Allerton, a little surprised by just how open she had been with him but grateful to her for it. "Given I won't be staying in England, I suppose it shouldn't matter to me a great deal, but..." Trailing off, Oliver's face twisted for a moment. "For whatever reason, I find myself wanting to fit in without any difficulty." One shoulder lifted in a half-shrug. "That's why I'm so grateful to Lady Georgiana."

A look of curiosity came into Lady Allerton's eyes. "Georgiana?" she repeated, looking at him in surprise. "What do you mean?"

"Oh." A quiet warning began to ring in Oliver's head,

but he thrust it aside easily enough. "Lady Georgiana has agreed to help me traverse this difficult sea," he said with a grin. "Since Lady Rutledge is quite worn out, you understand."

"I see." Lady Allerton did not look upset, only surprised. "That is good of her. But, then again, my sister-in-law has a very good heart."

"Yes," Oliver found himself saying with a good deal of fervor. "She does." A strange sensation began to flood his heart as he spoke these words, looking around as though he might see Lady Georgiana somewhere, as if she might have overheard him and would now be watching him.

She was nowhere to be seen.

Lady Allerton cleared her throat gently, catching Oliver a little off guard and making him realize not only what he had been thinking but just how obvious his thoughts must have been, given the look on Lady Allerton's face. A flush caught his cheeks, but he did not look away, shrugging with what was a slight air of embarrassment.

"And now, might we go through for a short performance?"

Oliver had been about to say something, something which, no doubt, would have been strangled with awkwardness and discomfiture, only for the voice of Lady Northcott to spread out across the room, catching everyone's attention. She was leading the way through the door into what must be the other room, and the guests were all milling towards her, leaving Oliver and Lady Allerton to do likewise.

Oliver was glad of the distraction, relieved he had not needed to say anything more, given what he would need to explain. It had surprised him just as much as it had Lady Allerton, since he had not meant to speak with such fervor nor such passion. Lady Georgiana was beautiful, of course, and he *did* find her heart to be one of kindness and compassion, but that was all there could be to it. He was to return to America soon, and to leave his heart behind here was something he knew would be incredibly foolish. And yet, the desire to leave, the desire to turn away and go back home had become considerably less welcoming. The thought of never seeing her again was a sharp pain that laced through his heart, leaving him almost breathless. How strange it was to feel such a strong emotion when he had been almost entirely unaware of it before!

The room was filled with guests, with a young lady seated at the pianoforte and another standing just to her left, either ready to help turn the pages of the music book or in preparation to sing. Oliver felt his spirits lift, wondering if they might be singing Christmas carols which he hoped very much to join in with. Moving quickly towards the back of the room, he caught sight of Lady Georgiana and found himself moving towards her.

Only to be intercepted by Lady Northcott.

"Ah, Mr. Lowell," she cooed, her eyes lifting to his face as the other guests continued to find places to sit. "Might you join me?" She gestured to two chairs, sitting slightly apart from the rest of the group, but a warning immediately began to ring in Oliver's mind as he and Lady Northcott stood to one side of the room.

"I am very sorry to disappoint, Lady Northcott," he said as quietly as he could. "But I am already promised to Lady Georgiana."

His hostess frowned immediately, her eyes darkening. "To Lady Georgiana?" she repeated, not looking anywhere but Oliver's face as though she was trying to decipher whether or not he was lying. "What can you mean?"

Spreading his hands, Oliver tried his best to look apologetic. "Lady Georgiana and I agreed to stand together for the performances this evening," he said with a small shrug. "I am afraid that I will know nothing about the pieces that will be performed and Lady Georgiana has offered to speak to me about each one of them." He smiled with what he hoped was a sorrowful look in his eyes. "Although I am very appreciative of your consideration."

Lady Northcott looked at him for a long time, her eyes glittering coldly. Oliver did not know what to do and merely held her gaze, fearing that if he lifted his eyes for even a moment, Lady Northcott would know he spoke untruths.

"I was hoping to have a private word with you at some point, Mr. Lowell," Lady Northcott said eventually, her tone brittle. "But perhaps Lady Georgiana has convinced you not to do so?"

Oliver pressed his lips together for a moment, considering what was the best thing to say. "Lady Georgiana has said nothing of the kind," he lied, not wanting to set any enmity between the ladies. "However, Lady Northcott, whilst I am very grateful to you for your friendship and your welcome, I must inform you that I have no intention of forming any particular bond with anyone while I am here in England." Praying that no one could overhear him but knowing he had to be honest with the lady, Oliver cleared his throat and lowered his tone, feeling awkward indeed. "I hope I have not insulted you."

Lady Northcott's cheeks had caught with a sudden fire, her eyes still fixed upon his own, but this time holding something akin to anger as she looked at him.

And then, she let out a long breath, turned her head away, and stepped to one side. "Good evening, Mr. Lowell," she said her voice quiet. "I hope you enjoy the musical performances."

Oliver did not know what to say and, therefore, chose to say nothing at all. He inclined his head and began to move forward into the room, seeing how the other guests had begun to settle themselves. Lady Georgiana was his goal, and he fixed his eyes on her, seeing how she glanced at him with evident concern. Perhaps she had seen Lady Northcott intercept him and feared what might have been said.

Someone jostled him hard, and he turned his head to see a footman staggering back, his hands both held up in apology and a stricken look on his face. Oliver, who had felt a sharp spike of anger, immediately threw such a feeling aside and gave the fellow a small smile, seeing the fear in the man's eyes and hating he had such power over the fellow. If he had learned anything about being here in England, it was that the servants could easily be dismissed over what was a tiny misdemeanor. He did not want to be that sort of gentleman and so shrugged, tried to smile reassuringly, and continued towards Lady Georgiana.

The footman bowed once, then twice, before backing away slowly, as if Oliver might turn back around at any moment to berate him, but Oliver was much too focused on hurrying towards Lady Georgiana so he would not be the last to find a place to stand in order to listen to the performances.

"You look quite relieved, Mr. Lowell."

He chuckled as he drew near Lady Georgiana, who was now smiling at him in welcome.

"I am glad to see you, that is all," he told her, seeing how she smiled but also how her eyes darted away for a moment. "I'm afraid that I might do or say something wrong, and then where would I be?"

Lady Georgiana rolled her eyes as her lips twitched. "Given we are at Lady Northcott's abode, I do not think that anything you said or did incorrectly would be taken as any insult," she said with a wry look in her eye. "It is Lady Northcott you must be careful of, Mr. Lowell."

Knowing she had seen him talking with their hostess, Oliver let out a long sigh. "I have been *very* careful," he told her quickly, as though he wanted her to be impressed by him. "When I first came in, I kept my conversation with Lady Northcott very brief indeed and then found Lady Allerton. And just now, I refused to sit with her."

"I am impressed!" Lady Georgiana laughed, pressing his arm for just a moment—a moment that flooded Oliver's heart with warmth. "You have done very well thus far, Mr. Lowell."

"Although," Oliver broke in, a small frown catching

his brow as he recalled just how Lady Northcott had looked, "I think that Lady Northcott was deeply upset with me."

"For refusing to sit with her?" Lady Georgiana asked, the smile gone from her face now. "Yes, I suppose she would be."

Oliver's frown deepened. "That is a little troubling."

Lady Georgiana shook her head firmly. "No, it is not," she said firmly. "Lady Northcott can be as upset as she wishes—you have no obligation to do as she asks. In making yourself clear, you have told her she can expect nothing from you and that, Mr. Lowell, is a very good thing indeed."

Oliver looked down into Lady Georgiana's face and found his heart beating a little faster as he smiled at her. She was quite remarkable, he decided, thinking he had found a true friend in Lady Georgiana. "I thank you," he said, exacting a bow that made Lady Georgiana beam with delight. "You have guided me correctly once again."

"Just as I said I would," Lady Georgiana reminded him with a small smile. "Now then, let us listen carefully to the first of our performers." She began to explain to him who the young lady was, and Oliver listened as carefully as he could whilst battling a strange desire to move closer to the lady, to draw nearer to her and to see her smiling face lifting up to his again. It was only when the music began he was able to push such a strange sensation away from him, focusing entirely on the beauty of the piece that filled the room as well as his heart. Closing his eyes, Oliver let out a long, slow breath, feeling a sense of contentedness fill his heart.

"It is quite lovely, is it not?" Lady Georgiana murmured when the guests began to applaud the young lady. "Lady Constance is one of the most accomplished young ladies in all of London. I am sure she will find a husband very soon."

Oliver smiled ruefully to himself. That was the purpose of such a performance, he realized. It was to prove the young lady's worth to any of the gentlemen that were present, to show to them just how wonderful she was.

"You look quite thoughtful, Mr. Lowell," Lady Georgiana commented quietly as the young lady prepared her second piece. "I did not think you would be so affected by something like this."

He shrugged one shoulder, not wanting to tell her everything that was in his thoughts at present. "Music can bring all manner of emotions to our hearts, can it not?" he remarked as Lady Georgiana looked up at him thoughtfully. "I am not saying I will need to pull a hankerchief from my pocket, but I will say that music, when it is performed well, can bring all manner of emotions to my heart."

Lady Georgiana smiled softly. "Very eloquent, Mr. Lowell," she remarked softly as he watched her with a warm expression on his face. "Very eloquent indeed."

There was no time to say more, for Lady Constance immediately began to play her second piece, although this time she sang along with it. The sound filled the room, swelling Oliver's heart, but he saw the slightly teasing look in Lady Georgiana's eye as she looked up at him. With a dramatic flourish, he made to pull his handkerchief from his pocket, intending to pretend he was using it to press away some tears from his eyes, only to feel something heavy tug at his kerchief.

Frowning, Oliver looked down at his pocket, expecting to see something there, but nothing was hanging over the side nor was it stuck in his handkerchief. He pulled his handkerchief free and felt something settle back down in his pocket again. Lady Georgiana was watching him with a confused expression on her face, and Oliver turned away slightly, feeling his heart thunder furiously.

His fingers touched something cold as he began to pull it out of his pocket. A shocked exclamation flew from his lips as he saw the emeralds began to sparkle in the light, staring down at the jewels in shock.

Lifting his eyes to Lady Georgiana, he saw her look first at the jewels and then up into his face. Her face had gone quite pale, her eyes searching his face.

"I didn't steal these," he whispered forcefully, his breath leaving his body in ragged gasps as he struggled to find a way to explain it. "I..." He shook his head, pressing the emeralds down into his pocket again.

The music came to a close, but Oliver remained where he was, half turned from the rest of the guests and grateful he was close to the wall. He could not understand it, could not begin to explain how such a thing could have been found in his possession.

A sudden scream ripped across the room, shattering the warm ambiance and making everyone turn towards Lady Northcott, who rose from her chair, one hand clutching at her throat.

Oliver went cold all over.

"Quickly."

He turned back, feeling his head begin to spin. Lady Georgiana was staring up at him fixedly as Lady Northcott began to wail.

"Give them to me," Lady Georgiana said firmly, her eyes holding his gaze with a steadiness that Oliver himself did not feel. "Give them to me at once, Mr. Lowell."

He could not move for a moment, too shocked, too stunned to do as she asked.

"Mr. Lowell," Lady Georgiana said again as Lady Northcott began to exclaim over her lost emerald necklace. "Give them to me at once. Before we are…" She trailed off, the fear in her eyes forcing him to act. With numb fingers, he grasped the emeralds and pulled them out of his pocket with as much stealth as he could. Lady Georgiana's hands were atop his in a moment, only for her to turn away and then begin to walk smartly away from him, her steps slow yet determined.

Oliver looked down. His hands were empty, the emeralds gone.

"We must conduct a search!" one gentleman cried, coming closer to Lady Northcott. "We must look for this necklace of yours, Lady Northcott." A small murmur ran around the room as the other gentlemen began to agree, whilst the ladies looked on in shock. "Surely, it cannot have gone far."

Lady Northcott sank into a chair, one hand over her eyes. "I only hope it has not been stolen," she said brokenly, sending a flurry of fear over Oliver's skin, feeling the hairs on the back of his neck stand up. "For if it has been, then I do not know what I shall do."

Oliver began to panic—not for himself but rather for Lady Georgiana, who now had the emerald necklace. What would happen if it was discovered she was the one carrying the necklace? Would she be thrown from society, forever doomed to carry the weight of guilt that ought not to be hers?

"I am sure that no one here would dare steal something from you," said one lady, coming closer to Lady Northcott, who held out one hand to her. "We are all friends, are we not?"

"We are," Lady Northcott answered with a slight sting in her voice. "Most of us are, at least." Her eyes turned towards Oliver, who knew at once what she intended. The way the footman had bumped into him, the anger in Lady Northcott's eyes now—it all made sense. He had rejected her and thus, she had done what she could to have him ejected from society. Either that or she expected him to plead with her somehow so that an arrangement could be made where he would pay for her silence.

Oliver was not about to allow her to do so.

"Here." He tugged off his coat, eliciting gasps from some of the ladies near to him. "If you would have your footmen search my pockets, Lady Northcott, I shall show to you that my other pockets," he gestured to his breeches, "are also quite empty." His voice rang around the room with a sense of strength and determination within it he was sure Lady Northcott had not expected.

"I may not be a part of your English society in every way, Lady Northcott, but I am no thief."

Lady Northcott's eyes glittered. "I thank you for your willingness to prove it," she said as one of the footmen plunged his hand into one of the coat pockets. Nothing was said for a few moments as she watched the footman closely, clearly expecting him to find something. Oliver stood quietly, feeling a sense of anger rising in his chest and silently praying that Lady Georgiana had found a place to hide the emeralds.

"There is nothing there, my lady."

Oliver accepted the coat back without a word, looking at Lady Northcott with a slightly raised eyebrow. Lady Northcott's face went a shade of scarlet, her eyes narrowed and brimming with rage. She was furious that her plan had not gone as she expected.

"Oh!"

A sudden exclamation from the other side of the room caught everyone's attention. A young lady gestured to the floor, in the corner of the room.

"Lady Northcott!" cried another, standing close to the first. "Might they be here? In the corner of the room?"

With another exclamation of surprise rippling about the room, Oliver watched as Lady Northcott rose from her chair, holding her head high as she moved towards the two young ladies, looking down at the floor and stepping back in evident astonishment.

Lady Georgiana had done well.

With a long breath of relief, Oliver watched as Lady Northcott began to express her gratitude to the two young ladies for spotting the emeralds, daring a glance back over her shoulder towards Oliver, who returned it with an easy smile. Very soon, the musical performances were continued, and whilst Oliver did not step into the company of Lady Georgiana again for the rest of the evening, he knew very well it was to her he had to be grateful. She had saved him, had not doubted him and had trusted he was not guilty. In acting as quickly as she had, she had saved him from ruin— saved both himself and Lord and Lady Rutledge, who would have borne the brunt of his shame in society. His heart swelled with warm regard for her once more, leaving him more determined than ever he would spend Christmas here in England, just so he could be in her company for a little longer. For the moment, nothing else seemed to matter.

CHAPTER SEVEN

"A very fine afternoon, Lady Georgiana, do you not think?"

Georgiana bit her lip, finding it quite impossible to respond to what was the very same comment Lord Poole had made only a few minutes ago. He was both dull and staid, clearly having no consideration for her comfort at the present moment. There was nothing in his conversation that caught her attention, no willingness to consider what she might be feeling at present but rather a self-interest that made her long to be free of his company.

"I have every intention of returning to the estate within the week," he informed her as the cold air began to nip at her cheeks. "The snow has begun to clear, I think, and I hope the roads will be adequate."

Georgiana said nothing, her heart beginning to fill with a deep heaviness that tugged her spirits all the lower. She did not want to marry Lord Poole, but her brother had made the arrangements and, given she had no other option, Georgiana had found herself betrothed to the gentleman without him even having to propose. When her brother had asked for her consent, Georgiana had hesitated for a moment—and in that moment, she had seen her brother frown, a deep concern in his eyes that spoke of anxiety and worry. Her heart had sunk down low, knowing that Lord Allerton had done what he could, had done his best to find an excellent match for her, and that if she refused to agree, then her brother might never again be able to find her a suitor—for news of her refusal would certainly make its way through society one way or another.

So, she had given her consent. Her brother had been quite delighted, and Georgiana had silently hoped she had not made a foolish mistake, worrying that Lord Poole was not the right character but fearing there would be no other choice for her. With her brother's previous financial difficulties, the *ton* still did not trust him fully, and, as such, only certain gentleman might be willing to consider her. She ought to be relieved, she told herself, that Lord Poole was not old and decrepit, or a widower with several children already. There were positive things about him, even if she was still quite disappointed, given all she had hoped for.

The difficulty was that, in the short time she had spent with him, Lord Poole was not improving himself upon her by any means. He might bear a good title and come from an excellent family, but that did not mean he had a good character. As far as she was concerned, he evidenced nothing but selfishness and considered nothing but his own interests. It was in his own interests to marry and thus, that was what he now intended to do.

It mattered very little to him whether or not *she* was contented, whether or not *she* had any concerns regarding their suitability. It was nothing more than a practical arrangement, and Georgiana could not help but feel as though she were nothing other than goods to be bartered.

"We will wed a week or two after Christmas," he told her, again making her realize she had no say whatsoever as to how things came about. "The banns, I hope, will be called this coming Sunday, but with the snow..." He shrugged as though it did not matter very much at all. "Once I receive word the banns have been called for the first Sunday, I will set a date for our marriage."

Georgiana let out a small, somewhat despondent breath. "I see," she muttered, a little sorrowfully. "And then we will reside at your estate?"

Lord Poole glanced at her as though she were being quite foolish. "Yes, of course," he told her with a shrug. "You will be expected to take on all the duties of the mistress of the house, and I shall continue with my affairs. Your rooms will be one side of the house, with mine on the other."

Georgiana frowned, glancing up at him. This was not the usual way of things, for a husband and wife usually had adjoining rooms, with one door between them. "To be so far apart is unusual," she said as he looked away from her. "Is there a particular reason as to why you wish such a thing?"

Lord Poole cleared his throat, a slight flush rising in his cheeks. "I do not like to be disturbed," he told her without once looking down into her face. "When I decide to come to you, then I shall do so quickly and without lingering."

Her cheeks heated as she held her gaze, seeing a small sense of awkwardness in his expression and wondering at it.

"And," he continued, clearing his throat again, "I wish to have privacy in my rooms, Lady Georgiana. That is something you should expect."

A sudden heavy weight flung itself down into her stomach, making her stagger. Lord Poole did not even notice, continuing on his with his long strides and never even glancing back at her. Georgiana forced herself to catch him, her pain beginning to rifle through her as she realized what her betrothed meant.

He meant he did not intend to remain solely hers. He already had other intentions, it seemed. Perhaps he already had others he did not wish to give up. Maids, even, who would give him whatever he wished whenever he wished it. If he chose to have a mistress, then she was to step aside and allow him to do so, even if she felt a great deal of pain over such a thing. It was something she ought to expect, he had told her, and yet the very thought of it sent such a sense of pain to her heart she could barely breathe.

Her mind filled with a vision of Mr. Lowell. Something within her just seemed to know he would never behave in such a manner, for he was honest and fair, with a good character and a clear sense of right and wrong. Would he marry and then seek out a mistress? Would he state he ought to be permitted to continue with any such liaisons without question? Or would he never even have permitted those liaisons to take place?

"I—I am not contented with such an arrangement," she said breathlessly as Lord Poole shot her an angry look. "That is not to my liking at all, Lord Poole."

A snort ripped from his throat, making her wince inwardly. "I care very little about what you like or what you do not," he told her, callously. "This is nothing more than an arrangement, Lady Georgiana. You will provide me with what I require, and, in return, I will provide you with what you require."

"And what is it you think I require?" she asked hotly, feeling a deep sense of anger begin to stir in her heart. "Loyalty? Fidelity?"

A scornful glance was dropped on her head. "Fidelity is not something you require, only something you would prefer," he told her without any opportunity for her to argue. "You *require* a good home, a husband, and a family. That is what every young lady requires, Lady Georgiana. And that is precisely what I intend to provide for you. If there is anything more you wish, that is nothing more than a preference, and thus, is not something I am obliged to give you."

Georgiana swallowed hard, feeling a ball of anger settling in her stomach and finding herself so furious, she could not find the words to speak. Lord Poole was not the sort of gentleman she wanted to marry, not when he cared so little for her and for their marriage. It was all about seeking his pleasures, his desires, and having no consideration for her whatsoever. Part of her wanted to return home and to demand that her brother bring this arrangement to an end, whilst the other part of her wanted to throw a stinging rebuttal into Lord Poole's face.

Not that she could do either, of course. As far as her brother was concerned, Lord Poole was an excellent match, and, as it looked on paper, he was. She had agreed to it also, had she not? Despite her concerns, which meant she had nothing but herself to blame for what would follow.

Despite the quiet urgings of your heart.

Georgiana closed her eyes for a moment, taking in a deep breath and steadying herself. Lord Poole, having given no consideration to her whatsoever, continued to walk forward, looking all about the park as though he might find something more interesting than his present company.

Georgiana walked a few steps behind him, glad for the quietness of the park and finding herself lost in thought. Thoughts that centered solely on Mr. Lowell. The soiree two nights ago had been something of a revelation, for not only had she had to make a decision as to whether or not Mr. Lowell could be trusted, but she had also then, thereafter, had to decide what she was to do. It had surprised her just how quickly she had acted, how swiftly she had decided he was *not* at fault. Whether or not it had been the look in his eyes, the shock in his expression, or the words of innocence that had sprung from his lips, she could not say—all she knew was there was something there that spoke to her heart. She had believed him, had trusted he had not stolen the necklace, and so had acted without so much as a second thought.

It had been simple enough to steal to the back of the room, very easy to drop the necklace to the floor in the corner of the room before stealing away again. Every eye had been on Lady Northcott, who had been putting on an excellent performance. When Georgiana had seen the anger in Lady Northcott's eyes as she had glared at Mr. Lowell, she had known for certain that her trust in him had not been misplaced. Lady Northcott was nothing more than a manipulative shrew who had taken Mr. Lowell's rejection of her very badly indeed and, thus, had attempted to have him thrown from society as a consequence. Upon reflection, Georgiana realized that Lady Northcott must have planned such a thing in advance, perhaps expecting Mr. Lowell to refuse her and devising a way to punish him. The dark scheming of Lady Northcott's mind frightened Georgiana, were she honest, and she was glad that Mr. Lowell had been spared any shame or embarrassment for something he had not done.

Her lips twisted together as she continued to consider Mr. Lowell. There was something about him that drew her to him. He did not know she had been watching him the very moment he had come into Lady Northcott's drawing-room, did not know that her eyes had fixed upon him, and watched closely as he spoke to Lady Northcott. Nor would he be aware of the relief that had flooded her as he had stepped away from their hostess and found Lady Allerton soon after. She had chosen to leave them to converse, not wanting to make her interest in the gentleman apparent, for even the awareness of it within her own heart had frightened her.

You cannot feel anything for Mr. Lowell, she told

herself firmly, looking up at the almost foreboding figure of Lord Poole, who was now walking ahead of her by quite a distance. *You are engaged.*

That did not bring her even the smallest surge of joy. Instead, she felt an ache building deep within her heart, felt her stomach twist and her throat begin to clog with a deep sense of regret. She could not let her heart become involved with another, not when she had already made her choice. Besides which, Mr. Lowell was to return to America soon, and she would never see him again for the rest of her life! It was foolish to even *consider* him, she told herself, her lips trembling at the swell of emotion that flooded her heart. For whatever reason, the thought of having to bid him farewell, of having to step away from him for good, brought her such pain she could not even allow her mind to dwell on it.

"This is to be the most miserable of Christmases," she muttered a tad ruefully as Georgiana forced her tears back. Normally, Christmas brought her a good deal of joy but, for this year, she found herself having no sense of happiness whatsoever. To be engaged was one thing, but to find herself betrothed to a gentleman who cared for no one but himself was quite another. There could be no happiness for her with this arrangement, Georgiana knew, but she had made her decision. Mr. Lowell would return to America, she would remain here, and their lives would continue in very different directions.

"Ah, Lady Georgiana! I thought that must be you!"

Her heart turned over in her chest as she started with surprise, having not seen the very man she had been considering now approaching her from the left.

"Mr....Mr. Lowell," she stammered, aware of how heat rushed up into her face and left her blushing. "I did not see you."

"Apparently." His grin was easy but only added to her sense of embarrassment. "It is very cold for you to be walking out today. Is there nobody with you?" He chuckled as Georgiana ducked her head. "I thought that was most improper."

Georgiana pressed her lips together tightly, her stomach twisting with nervousness. She would have to tell Mr. Lowell about Lord Poole, of course, but something within her feared for his reaction. There was an awkwardness there, a tension she had not felt before. It was as if she wanted to hide her betrothal from him, wanted to pretend she was as free as he believed her to be. And yet the truth stuck out starkly before her, making her drag in air as she tried to find the right words to say.

"I—I am not here alone, Mr. Lowell," she began, seeing how he looked at her in surprise. "This gentleman is accompanying me." She gestured hopelessly towards Lord Poole, who had not so much as glanced over his shoulder to see where she might be. "Lord Poole," she said dully.

Mr. Lowell blinked in surprise, glancing from Georgiana's face to Lord Poole and then back again. "He doesn't seem to be doing a good job of walking alongside you," he said with a frown. "I thought a gentleman was meant to take great care to always pay great attention to the lady in question."

Georgiana wanted to turn away, such was her embarrassment, but forced a smile to her face instead. "You are quite correct there, Mr. Lowell," she said somewhat awkwardly. "Lord Poole is often...distracted by his thoughts, as you see him here at the present moment." She gestured behind her. "And my maid is also present, as you can see."

Mr. Lowell's frown did not fade. "That is rather unorthodox still," he said with a slight shake of his head. "Rude, in fact." Tilting his head, he looked at her sharply. "He is not attempting to court you, I hope!" he exclaimed, a sudden mirth filling his eyes. "I fear he is doomed to fail otherwise!"

Georgiana did not smile and, as she looked back into the warm hazel eyes of Mr. Lowell, she felt her heart squeeze with an overwhelming pain that had her wanting to cry out aloud.

"He is not courting me, no," she said softly as Mr. Lowell's eyes began to widen with surprise. "He is my betrothed."

For some moments, neither of them said anything more. Mr. Lowell stared at Georgiana as though he expected her to say something more, to explain herself in a manner that made sense. Georgiana did not know what to do nor even where to look, her gaze unable to find a place to settle and rest.

"I—I did not know..." Mr. Lowell cleared his throat gruffly, his eyes on the ground as he attempted to regain his composure. "I mean to say, Lady Georgiana, that I offer you my hearty congratulations." This was accompanied by a swift bow, although his hand reached out towards her, and Georgiana found herself giving him her hand without even a momentary hesitation. "I am sure Lord Poole will be an excellent husband to you."

"Thank you." Georgiana hated that her voice was so thin, so pained, and with a sense of sorrow within it, but there was nothing she could do to prevent such a thing from occurring. She was not happy with her engagement, was not at all satisfied nor content, but there was nothing she could do. She could not even voice her upset, for it would be entirely improper to state such a thing in front of Mr. Lowell.

"Will you remain in London for a time still?" he asked, a slight catch in his voice. "Or are you to wed before Christmas?"

Her throat worked for a moment, unable to force a smile to her lips. "Lord Poole has a townhouse here, of course, and his brother resides in London also, but he is very eager to return to his estate. We will marry shortly after Christmas, I believe, but at my brother's estate rather than Lord Poole's."

There came a short, terse silence where Georgiana did not dare to even look into Mr. Lowell's face for fear of what she might see there.

"You will be very happy, I hope," Mr. Lowell answered, his hand still holding hers and, as she finally lifted her gaze to look into his eyes, taking a small step forward. "You deserve to have the kindest, most considerate of husbands, Lady Georgiana, for your heart is gentle, sweet, and compassionate. It is rare to find someone as considerate as you are, Lady Georgiana. And I say this with the knowledge that I myself have been blessed in my friendship with you."

Georgiana wanted to say something in return, wanted to tell him she appreciated his words and she did not want to be married to Lord Poole, but the words stuck in her throat. As Mr. Lowell lifted her hand to his mouth, Georgiana felt herself tremble and wondered if he felt it. His eyes caught hers for a moment, just as his lips touched her skin in a gentle kiss.

Georgiana's blood burned with fire as she shuddered violently with the depths of emotions that slammed straight into her, almost forcing her to step closer. Mr. Lowell must have felt it also, for he lifted his head and looked straight into her eyes, his hand tight on hers, his fingers caressing where his lips had just been. There was nothing she could say, nothing that would make any sense, at least, for all sense had been knocked from her, leaving her breathless and giddy.

"Lady Georgiana, I—"

"Just what is the meaning of this?"

Georgiana stepped back almost at once, only just hearing the frantic whispering of her maid, who must have been trying to get her attention for at least a minute or two. Praying she did not look flustered, she looked up at Lord Poole and stepped nimbly in front of Mr. Lowell, so that her betrothed could not flail a fist out towards him, should he be so inclined.

"Lord Poole," she said as firmly as she could despite the trembling that still ran through her. "This is Mr. Lowell, a *dear* friend of Lady Allerton and the cousin of Lord Rutledge. He has come to England from Boston, to visit his cousin." She saw Lord Poole's angry expression begin to fade as the names she had mentioned took hold of his senses. "You have not been introduced, I think?" She took a deft sidestep and let the two gentlemen greet each other, feeling all of a tremble still at whatever it was that occurred within her heart. "Mr. Lowell had only just heard news of our engagement and was congratulating me."

Lord Poole did not look entirely convinced but gave Mr. Lowell a terse nod, eyeing him suspiciously.

"My hearty congratulations," Mr. Lowell said with happiness in his voice Georgiana was sure he did not feel. "And are you to wed before Christmas?"

Lord Poole sniffed and looked away. "Surely you know there is not enough time," he said with a hint of arrogance in his voice. "There are not enough Sundays for the banns to be called. No, we shall wed soon after Christmas. Just as soon as I can manage it, in fact." This was said with one sharp eye being placed firmly on Georgiana, making her squirm inwardly as if Lord Poole could see inside her heart and knew precisely what she was thinking. His eyes swiveled back to Mr. Lowell, who was now wearing an expression of cool disinterest. "No doubt you will be back to America before then."

Georgiana's heart lurched. It was a clear set down, a tangible warning towards Mr. Lowell, and Mr. Lowell seemed to understand it.

"I fear I shall, yes," he said with only a small glance towards Georgiana. "I will be returning to Boston very soon. Good afternoon to you both." He smiled tightly at Georgiana, inclined his head towards Lord Poole, and then turned on his heel, walking away smartly and leaving nothing but terse silence growing between Georgiana and Lord Poole.

Georgiana turned to her betrothed, seeing the man's sharp eyes following Mr. Lowell as if he expected him to turn back around and rush towards Georgiana. "There was no need for such a remark," she said before she could stop herself. "Mr. Lowell was only being polite."

Much to her shock, Lord Poole grasped her arm tightly, twisting it upwards in a deeply painful motion.

"Do not ever consider that you have any right to tell me how I ought to behave," he said harshly, his face only inches from hers and an anger swelling within them that sent a surge of fear deep into Georgiana's soul. "Mr. Lowell is far too interested in you, I think. You will stay away from him."

Despite her fear, despite her upset, Georgiana wrenched her arm away from Lord Poole with an effort, feeling the burning pain in her arm where his fingers had squeezed. "You will find, Lord Poole, that I am quite able to make my own judgments when it comes to who I should or should not speak to," she said with more harshness than she had intended but with a growing determination in her heart. "Mr. Lowell was only being polite. He is a friend of my sister-in-law's, and I have no intention of stepping away from him merely because you wish it."

A hand reached out and crashed across her face, sending her spiraling backward. The pain was one shock, but the realization of what he had done came as quite another. Georgiana pressed one hand to her face, aware of just how violently she was shaking. Snow began to fall lightly around them, making for a beautiful scene, but one that brought Georgiana no peace. She looked back at her betrothed, seeing how red his face was, how angry his eyes were, and felt herself shudder violently.

Lord Poole was not a man to be trifled with.

"You will never again speak to Mr. Lowell," he told her, his voice hard. "If you do, then I shall ruin him and have him flung back to America by even his closest cousins." The darkness in his words told Georgiana he had every intention of doing just as he said, making her realize that her betrothed *had* seen something in how Mr. Lowell had taken her hand. Or perhaps he had seen it in her face as he had come back towards them both.

"Return to the carriage." His voice was harsh, one long finger pointed out towards Georgiana. "Now."

Georgiana wanted to stand her ground, wanted to tell him she would not be bullied into submission by fear, but the look in his eyes told her otherwise. With a silent scream lodged in her throat, she turned around slowly and began to trudge back towards the carriage, one hand pressed at her cheek where Lord Poole had hit her. There was no strength left within her now, no courage to do or to say what was required. Instead, all she felt was afraid.

Is this the man I am to marry? she asked herself as the maid pulled the carriage door open for her, her eyes wide with fright as she glanced back at Lord Poole. *A man who would strike me any time I behave in an incorrect fashion, according to his judgments?* Her future grew all the darker, leaving her trapped between fear and duty, between expectation and trepidation. And as Lord Poole sat opposite her, his eyes narrowed and fixed on hers,

Georgiana felt herself begin to shake with both fright and the shock of what had occurred. She could not get her thoughts into coherent order, could not begin to work out what she ought to do next.

All there was now was swirling blackness and shadows with long, thin fingers, holding her tight against them as she gave up her strength and allowed the darkness to take hold.

CHAPTER EIGHT

"Would you like to tell me if there is a reason for your despondency?"

Oliver grimaced, pushing around his food on his plate and aware of the sharp look his cousin was giving him. "Your concern is greatly appreciated, but I am quite well."

Lady Rutledge laughed, a sharp look in her eye. "I cannot think you believe you can fool me so easily," she said with a small, wry smile. "There is something on your mind, and I would like very much to know what it is so you stop moping around this house when it is very soon to be Christmas!" She set her fork down carefully before looking at him again. "In ten days' time, in fact," she said as though this ought to please him. "We shall have the Yule log brought in very soon, and the greenery will be spread across the house in decoration on Christmas Eve." A long, contented sigh escaped her as she sat back inelegantly in her chair. "And I do hope you have a gift for me," she finished with a small, teasing smile. "It will be quite disastrous if you do not."

Oliver cleared his throat, set down his fork, and looked his cousin straight in the eye. "I think I might return to Boston," he said heavily. "I think it is time that I did so."

Lady Rutledge blinked rapidly, her face falling at once. "Whatever can you mean?" she exclaimed, sitting bolt upright. "To leave before Christmas? Why should you do such a thing?"

"Because I..." Oliver trailed off, not wanting to explain his reasons for returning home. To do so would be to admit to his cousin he was half in love with Lady Georgiana and that seeing her some days ago with Lord Poole —who, he then discovered was Lady Georgiana's betrothed—had quite taken the heart from him. He did not want to risk seeing her with him again, for fear of what it would do to his spirits.

"Because?" Lady Rutledge repeated, looking at him steadily. "Come now, Lowell, you must tell me the truth. It is most unlike you to be so quiet. You appeared to be enjoying every day here in London, and now you say you wish to return home?" Lady Rutledge now appeared to be quite distressed, for her eyes were somewhat glassy, and her forehead puckered with a frown. "Please, will you not tell me the truth?"

Sighing heavily, Oliver looked across the table at his cousin, perhaps a little relieved that Lord Rutledge was absent this evening. He would not even consider speaking honestly were he here—and yet there was still a reluctance on Oliver's part. To say any such thing aloud would be to admit even to himself the depths of what he now felt for Lady Georgiana. Depths he had only just discovered when he had looked into her eyes and felt her pulled away from him.

"Lowell, please." Lady Rutledge was leaning forward now, her eyes holding a desperation, an urge to understand. "What is it?"

Oliver let out another long breath, shaking his head to himself and closing his eyes. "I fear, my dear cousin, that I am quite lost."

"Lost?" Lady Rutledge repeated, clearly about to question what such a statement meant, only for Oliver to hold up his hand, silencing her. He needed to take his time, to speak carefully and slowly so she might understand and so he himself explained himself properly.

"I am lost due to my heart," he told her, looking across the table and seeing how her eyes flared. "I think that I might be in love."

Lady Rutledge stared at him for a long moment before a small exclamation left her lips, forcing her to clap her hands across her mouth to silence herself.

"I know," Oliver said heavily, aware of how heat was beginning to crawl up his spine but not feeling any embarrassment at having admitted as such. "What makes it worse is the lady in question is betrothed."

Another squeak left Lady Rutledge's mouth, her eyes rounding all the more.

"But you cannot!" Words began to tumble from her lips, her hands now in two tight fists as she slammed them down on the table. "You cannot be in love with someone who is already betrothed, Lowell!"

Another sigh. "I am well aware of that, my dear cousin," he said wryly, shooting her a hard look that had her blushing. "It is not my choice to feel such a way, I promise you. And I have only just now realized just how strongly I feel for her." Rubbing one hand over his face, he shook his head. "It is foolish, I know. I have never had any intention of falling in love with anyone, particularly not someone from England when I live in America!" A harsh laugh left his lips as Lady Rutledge continued to stare at him in shock. "If I return home, then perhaps these feelings will die quickly. I don't want to feel them any longer."

Lady Rutledge shook her head slowly, looking at him with a graveness in her expression that Oliver could not fully comprehend.

"You cannot run from such things," she said slowly as Oliver rolled his eyes at her remark. "You can consider me foolish if you like, Lowell, but I know that your feelings will not simply fade away because you have left London. Rather, they will grow until you are quite tormented by being so far from her...whoever she is." A flicker of interest in her eyes, she continued to speak. "What if there is a chance for you to find happiness with this young lady?"

"There isn't," Oliver answered emphatically. "You told me yourself it is quite terrible if a lady ends her engagement."

"If she 'cries off,'" Lady Rutledge corrected, a little primly. "Yes, there is that. But if you are to go to America, would she not consider going with you? There would be no shame in that. Indeed, in doing so, she would leave all of her shame here."

"I do not even know if she cares for me," he answered darkly. "I cannot be sure."

"It is not a risk you would dare to take?" came the reply, making his eyes dart away as the question tore at him. "A risk that might bring you a different future from the one you have laid out before you at present?"

Oliver wanted to shake his head, wanted to say there was no possibility of Lady Georgiana ever considering him or thinking of coming to America to join him, but the memory of the look in her eyes when he'd kissed her hand made him start. There had been a flash of heat there, a spark of something she had been trying desperately to keep hidden. He had felt her trembling, had seen her taking a small step forward towards him as though she wanted to keep away but could not bring herself to do so. He had felt something change between them then, had felt as though the very air they breathed was filled with sparks, sending lightning through him as he had looked into her eyes. The memory of his lips on her gentle skin sent a flurry of warmth into his heart, beginning to feel it burning with hope. A tiny hope, yes, but hope, nonetheless.

"You cannot give up so easily," Lady Rutledge said firmly. "I have never pretended that I cared for Lord Rutledge when we first met, but I have been blessed with a marriage where deep feelings have been allowed to grow and flourish—to the point that I could not consider life without him." Her smile gentled, her eyes holding an understanding that Oliver could almost feel. "Surely you do not want to simply give up and return home without even attempting to see what might become of things between you?"

Oliver shook his head, looking up at his cousin ruefully. "You are meant to be the epitome of propriety," he reminded her as she chuckled. "You have guided me for these last few months, you have berated me, corrected me, and taught me—and now you are encouraging me to ask a young lady to break off her engagement and practically elope to America with me?"

Lady Rutledge blushed at this remark but did not deny it. "There are times when propriety must fade away in place of what is best for one's heart," she said quietly, her gaze settled. "I am glad you have told me, Lowell—although you have not mentioned the lady's name?" She looked at him enquiringly, but Oliver shook his head.

"I would prefer to keep her name to myself for the moment, cousin," he told Lady Rutledge. "Just to ensure her safety. After all," he continued, his brow furrowing as he recalled just how brusque and angry Lord Poole had been, "her betrothed does not appear to be the kindest of men."

"All the more reason for you to offer her your heart in his place," Lady Rutledge said decisively. "Now, when will you see her again? This evening?" She shot him a hard look. "Now I well understand why you have kept away from society these last two nights!"

Oliver grinned wryly. "Yes, now you know," he admitted, a little guiltily. "This evening, perhaps? Where are we to go?"

Lady Rutledge smiled. "We have an invitation to

Lady Moncrieff's Christmas ball," she answered. "It will have almost everyone from within the *ton* present, I am sure. Your lady in question will be there. I have no doubt."

His spirits a good deal more buoyed than before, Oliver smiled and sat back in his chair, all thoughts of returning to America now gone from his mind. "Good," he answered, seeing Lady Rutledge smile. "Then this evening, I will attend this Christmas ball."

"And I will pray you will be given the opportunity to speak to her," Lady Rutledge said decisively. "And you will tell me her name thereafter!"

Lady Moncrieff's Christmas ball was quite lovely, Oliver reflected, looking around the ballroom and feeling his spirits lift all the more. The ballroom was very busy indeed, but the townhouse was one of the finest he had ever seen, with a small balcony overlooking the ballroom itself. Lady Moncrieff was the widow of the Marquess of Moncrieff and clearly enjoyed spending time in good company, for the ball was a very lavish affair. There were footmen carrying silver trays of what appeared to be glasses of champagne and glasses of brandy. The fire in the middle of the room burned, the candelabras adding extra brightness to duller parts of the room. Oliver smiled to himself as he saw the mistletoe bough, seeing how couples danced past it, with one or two stopping for a moment. The lady would blush, the gentleman would reach up to pick a berry from the bough, and then would steal a kiss from the lady in return. Some were bolder than others, he noticed, with some pressing their lips to a lady's cheek whilst others kissed the lady full on the mouth.

A sudden idea struck him, sending a tremor through him. He would know for certain how Lady Georgiana felt should she allow him to kiss her under the mistletoe bough. It would be quite acceptable, he would be doing nothing improper, and yet her reaction to his kiss would give him all the answers he required.

A sudden, frantic urge caught him, and Oliver found himself practically running towards the few steps that would lead him into the ballroom directly. He had not seen Lady Georgiana as yet, but surely she would be here! This was one of the most extravagant balls of the Season, his cousin had said, and everyone of importance would be present.

Aware he was being a trifle rude in how he pushed through the crowd, Oliver let his eyes rove from one side to the other in search of her, his heart beating at a furious, frantic pace. A little to his right, he saw the mistletoe bough and felt his stomach twist with eager anticipation.

"Good gracious, Mr. Lowell!"

Oliver came to a dead stop, seeing how Lady Allerton held up one hand with the other hand clutching a glass of champagne. She stepped back from him just in time, with only the tiniest drop of champagne escaping from the glass. He had practically walked straight into her.

"I apologize, Lady Allerton," Oliver said at once, a little flustered. "I am looking for Lady Georgiana."

Looking into her face hopefully, he saw how her expression clouded.

"Lady Georgiana is..." the lady sighed and looked away. "She *is* present this evening, Mr. Lowell, but I fear you will not find her in good spirits."

Oliver frowned. "Is something wrong?"

"Who can say?" Lady Allerton replied with a shrug of her shoulders. "Lady Georgiana will say nothing. Her eyes are downcast, her expression sorrowful, but she will say not a word."

A deep sense of worry began to climb up Oliver's throat. "I should speak to her," he said half to himself as he looked around the room for her. "I do hope that after our last conversation, she has not thought ill of me." Perhaps, he realized, she had been upset with what he had done in kissing her hand, or perhaps Lord Poole had berated her after he had left. Either way, he prayed he was not the cause of her upset.

"I—I must ask, Mr. Lowell," Lady Allerton said hesitantly as he returned his attention to her. "Was anything said between you at this last meeting? Or did Lord Poole say anything to upset her?"

Now it was Oliver's turn to hesitate. He saw Lady Allerton's eyes flicker as if she had known that *something* had occurred but did not quite know what that something was.

"Lord Poole was a little upset that I was speaking to Lady Georgiana," he admitted slowly, making certain not to mention the gentleman had seen him kissing Lady Georgiana's hand. "He came over almost at once, and had it not been for Lady Georgiana's introductions, I think he might well have lashed out at me."

Lady Allerton's eyes flared wide.

"Not that he did, of course," Oliver continued quickly, not wanting to give a false impression of the gentleman. "Once Lady Georgiana had introduced me, he seemed...less inclined towards violence."

Pressing her lips together hard, Lady Allerton shook her head mutely.

"I will say he did not think well of me, however," Oliver finished with a small, sad smile. "I am not a gentleman, of course, and he made his disdain quite apparent."

Lady Allerton looked away. "I am sorry for that," she said quietly, clearly a little embarrassed. "Lord Poole appeared to be an excellent gentleman, if not a little cold in his manner, and both Lord Allerton and I thought him a suitable match for Lady Georgiana."

"But why does she need one?" Oliver found himself asking, earnestly. "Why should you push her into something like that? Why not let her choose her suitor?"

Lady Allerton's eyes grew sad. "Because the *ton* does not yet trust my husband," she said making Oliver stare at her in surprise. "It is not because he is deemed to be devious or the like, but rather that his monies were once very low indeed." She lifted one shoulder. "That is why he had to marry me. The ladies of the *ton* were not about to look to a well-titled but poor Earl—so, therefore, an arrangement was made, and I was sent over here."

"I see," Oliver said slowly, a little overcome with surprise.

"The *ton* does not forget things easily," Lady Allerton

continued, with a sigh. "The gentlemen of the *beau monde* will not consider Lady Georgiana for fear that her brother will have no good dowry for her."

"And that is considered to be important?" Oliver asked, a little disbelieving. "You are telling me that a gentleman might find Lady Georgiana to be quite wonderful in every way, but due to her smaller dowry—or due to the fear that her brother will not provide one for her—he wouldn't consider her?"

Lady Allerton nodded, her expression grim. "That is it precisely, Mr. Lowell," she told him, making him shake his head in astonishment. "It is all the more difficult to understand when you realize that Lady Georgiana herself had nothing to do with it."

Oliver felt something within him tighten as a faint anger brushed over his skin. He was angry with the *ton*, angry with their foolish ways, and their demeaning of others based on very little indeed. He was angry with Lord Poole for treating Lady Georgiana as though she had no right to stop and speak to a friend whilst he himself strode ahead of her, clearly giving her very little attention. And he was angry with himself for allowing his heart to become filled with her when he knew he could do nothing about such feelings.

"Oh, there she is!" Lady Allerton gestured somewhere over Oliver's right shoulder, and he turned to see her being led from the floor by a gentleman he did not know. The gentleman was smiling down at Lady Georgiana and, whilst she smiled back at him, there was no sense of true happiness that came from her. Instead, he thought, there was something guarded about her expression, something hidden, something held back. He watched her carefully as the gentleman brought her back to Lady Allerton, seeing the widening of her eyes as she saw him standing there.

"Good evening, Lady Georgiana," he said bowing quickly. "And good evening to you also, sir."

The gentleman grinned, bowed, and excused himself almost at once, claiming he had to go in search of his next dance partner. Lady Georgiana stood quietly for some minutes, looking from right to left as though expecting someone else to come to greet her.

"Did you enjoy your dance with Lord Ferguson?" Lady Allerton asked as a small silence grew between Oliver and Lady Georgiana. "He is an excellent dancer by all accounts."

Lady Georgiana shrugged delicately. "He is a very good dancer, yes," she admitted, her voice soft but her eyes not even drawing near to Oliver. "I was to dance the waltz with Lord Hunter, but I have only just now seen him leaving the ballroom." Her expression darkened for a moment. "Most likely, he will be making his way to the card room."

Oliver seized the opportunity. "Then I should be glad to dance with you in his place," he said at once, bowing quickly. "Shall we make our way to the floor, Lady Georgiana?" Putting out his hand, he looked down into her face only to see how her eyes darted away as if he were chasing her. She looked trapped, her hands clasped tightly in front of her, her shoulders hunched and her head down.

"Lady Georgiana?"

His voice was softer now, trying to pull her out of whatever this difficulty was, but Lady Georgiana did not appear to want to be pulled free. Instead, she shook her head, making Lady Allerton stare at her in surprise.

"You don't want to dance with me?" he asked, lapsing back into less formal speech for a moment, such was his surprise. "Why not? What have I done wrong?"

"Nothing!" Lady Georgiana's eyes shot to his and she took an involuntary step forward, her hands unclenched and reaching for him—only for her to realize what she was doing, drop her hands to her sides, and squeeze her eyes shut. A ripple of pain ran over her expression, and it was all Oliver could do not to reach forward and take her hands, wondering why she appeared so upset.

"Georgiana," Lady Allerton said softly, clearly worried for her sister-in-law. "Whatever is the matter?"

Lady Georgiana swallowed hard, opened her eyes, and let her shoulders lower down slowly. "Nothing is wrong," she answered, seeming very calm. Her eyes caught on something behind him, watching it closely for some moments, and it took all of Oliver's strength not to turn around to look at whatever it was.

"Mr. Lowell." Her eyes turned back to his, looking into his face with a steadiness that surprised her. "I would be glad to accept your offer of a dance."

"Oh." For a moment, he stood there, mute, only to realize what she had said. Such had been the swiftness of her change of heart it threw him for a moment or two. It was only when she reached out a hand he collected himself, clearing his throat gruffly and taking her hand in his. She went willingly, a gentle smile on her face that did not quite reach her eyes. When the music began, Oliver took her in his arms and felt his heart roar with a new, fresh passion that burned all through him. Yet, as he let his gaze rest on her troubled expression, he felt something begin to steal the happiness from him.

"Something is troubling you, Lady Georgiana," he said unequivocally, as they began to spin around the floor. "Won't you tell me what it is?"

Lady Georgiana swallowed hard, her lips trembling as her eyes darted away. "I—I have nothing to tell you," she said softly. "Everything is quite all right."

"But I do not believe you," he told her quietly, seeing how they came near to the mistletoe bough, forced to slow as some couples stopped for a moment so the gentleman might pull a berry from its branches. "Something is troubling you, and I am afraid it has something to do with me."

Her eyes shot to his. "In what way, Mr. Lowell?" she asked a trifle tersely. "I do not understand what you mean."

"Since our meeting with Lord Poole, your sister-in-law says you are quieter and almost sorrowful," he told her, seeing Lady Georgiana bite her lip as they twirled around the floor again. Leaving the mistletoe bough behind, Oliver thought to make another turn around the floor before approaching it again. "Was that my doing, Lady Georgiana?" he asked softly. "Did I offend Lord Poole?"

She shuddered violently, to the point he almost stopped dancing, but as she tightened her hands in his, he was practically forced to continue.

"Lord Poole was not very happy with what he witnessed, Mr. Lowell," Lady Georgiana said, her voice so quiet he had to strain to hear her. "Consequently, I am not to be seen with you again."

The truth was given to him so quickly, it took Oliver a few minutes before he was able to comprehend what Lady Georgiana had said. His steps began to slow, his eyes fixed solely on her, but Lady Georgiana would not so much as look at him. Her head lowered, her eyes tight to his chest so she would not have to look up into his face, despite Oliver's unspoken desperation she do so.

"Why are you dancing with me, then?" he asked quietly, his chest tight with anger. "What if he sees this?"

"He will not," Lady Georgiana answered as they neared the mistletoe bough again. "He is gone from the room."

Oliver wanted to close his eyes in frustration, realizing that *this* was why Lady Georgiana had been willing to dance with him in what had been a very quick change of heart.

"I am not staying away from you for my sake," Lady Georgiana said urgently, her stormy eyes now lifted to his, "but for yours."

"For my sake?" he repeated, somewhere between anger and confusion. "What do you mean, Lady Georgiana?"

Her throat worked for a moment, but she did not look away. Oliver realized they had come to the mistletoe bough, and reaching up, plucked one of the berries from it before stepping aside. Lady Georgiana was out of his arms now, the music continuing, but with the crush of couples all trying to get near to the mistletoe bough, it was easy enough for them both to leave the dance floor without being noticed. Practically cradling the berry in his hand, Oliver took Lady Georgiana's hand and drew her a little further into the shadows, knowing that most of the *ton*'s attention would be on those who still remained, watching to see who might steal a kiss.

"What do you mean, Lady Georgiana?" he asked again, coming to a stop and turning so she faced him, her eyes now a little glassy with what he supposed to be tears. "I do not understand."

Lady Georgiana closed her eyes tightly, and, to his horror, a single tear ran down her cheek. Unable to help himself, he reached out and brushed it away gently, feeling his heart racing as he touched her smooth skin. The way his whole body reacted to her nearness reminded him of just how much he had come to care for Lady Georgiana, even though he did not want to feel anything for her. It could not be denied. It was there, deep within himself, and no longer something he could hide from himself.

"Lord Poole has said that, should we be seen together, then he will make sure to ruin you," Lady Georgiana whispered, her eyes still closed but seeming to lean into his hand as he ran it down her cheek. "He states he will have you return to America in disgrace and that your shame—whatever it is he intends to do—will touch even Lord and Lady Rutledge." Her voice began to shake with the depths of emotion that was so obviously in her heart. "It is not my desire to push you away, Mr. Lowell, but I can see no other choice."

Everything in Oliver wanted to go and find Lord Poole and to shake him senseless for making such a cruel demand. And, at the same time, he wanted to pull Lady Georgiana into his arms and tell her just how much he had come to care for her, how appreciative he was of her willingness to protect him.

"That man is not worthy of you," he told her firmly, aware of the surprise in her expression as she opened her eyes to look at him. "He is a cruel man, Lady Georgiana. Why would you marry him?"

"I—I have no other choice," she whispered, a little sorrowfully. "My brother—"

"Surely there is someone here within the *ton* who will overlook your brother's financial difficulties!" he exclaimed as Lady Georgiana shook her head miserably. "Good gracious, gentlemen here are truly more foolish than I first thought!" He caught himself, hearing his voice rising and knew he had to remain as quiet as he could. "What I mean to say is, Lady Georgiana, that to base one's marriage on the money one's wife can bring to it does not say much about the state of one's heart." Taking a small step closer, he looked down into her eyes and felt his heart ache for her. "Lady Georgiana, I do not care about money." It was not what he had intended to say, not what he *wanted* to say, but there was something about speaking with such honesty that felt right, that lifted his spirits. Lady Georgiana's eyes flared as she looked up at him, her face a little pale.

"I have this." Holding up the mistletoe berry, he looked into her eyes questioningly. "I think I am right about what is expected."

A tiny smile caught the corner of her mouth as a slight flush rose in her cheeks. "You are not *quite* correct, sir," she told him, a slight lilt to her voice. "The kiss is meant to be taken under the mistletoe bough."

Oliver's voice was husky. "Then you will not grant me it?"

Lady Georgiana hesitated, her eyes searching his. "It is not that I want to stay away from you, Mr. Lowell," she told him, stepping forward and putting one hand on his chest, sending sparks all through him. "I want only to protect you and your cousin."

He nodded, thinking to himself he had never met a creature as wonderful as this. "And I, Lady Georgiana, do not intend to ruin whatever it is you have planned for your future, only to suggest there might be a different path for you to take."

Her shoulders slumped, a despondent look in her eyes. "What different path might that be?" she asked him sorrowfully. "I can see no other way forward."

Oliver acted at once, pressing his hand over hers and seeing how her head lifted at once. "America is very far away," he told her, softly. "Far away from all the scandal and the ruin that might come from following one's heart." He could see from the look in her eyes she understood what he was offering her but did not want to press her into making a decision straight away. "I am not afraid of Lord Poole," he finished, holding up the mistletoe berry before pressing it into her hand. "Nor should you be."

Lady Georgiana acted before he had a chance to think. Her lips were pressed to his, her hand about his neck and her fingers in his hair. Such was his surprise it took Oliver a moment to collect himself, to rest his hands on her waist, to pull her lightly to him—and then she stepped away from him and was gone. Not another word was spoken, not even another look exchanged. The imprint of her lips on his was all that lingered, making Oliver sigh with both contentment and frustration as he tried to find her in the crowd, wondering if he had just made everything worse by doing such a thing as stealing a kiss.

But I do not regret it, he told himself, firmly. *For the rest of my life, I will never regret stealing a Christmas kiss from Lady Georgiana. It was a magical moment, thanks to the mistletoe.*

His heart lifted just a little, although his anger and his upset over Lord Poole still remained. With dulled spirits, Oliver turned quietly around, keeping to the side of the room as he made his way through the ballroom and out towards the carriages.

It was time for him to go home.

CHAPTER NINE

Georgiana held her breath as Lord Poole moved slowly around the room, his eyes never quite landing on her. Ever since Mr. Lowell had kissed her last evening, she had felt herself growing more and more anxious, afraid of what Lord Poole would say when he next came to call. Something within her feared he knew what had occurred between herself and Mr. Lowell, afraid he had discovered it either by his own eyes or by hearing it from another. At Christmastime, such kisses were whispered and talked about at length, but there were never any lasting consequences, given it was Christmastime, and the mistletoe bough practically demanded that kisses were given and received.

Although perhaps with a little less passion than was displayed last evening.

Heat rose in Georgiana's face, but she pushed the feeling of embarrassment away at once. There was nothing wrong with what she had done, she told herself. She had given in to her feelings of affection towards Mr.

Lowell and had done something that had felt quite natural. It was a magical moment. In fact, it had over-whelmed her senses, had taken everything from her, and had sent spirals of affection deep into her heart.

Mr. Lowell was not about to be removed from her heart easily.

Georgiana had barely slept the previous evening, both thoroughly confused and a little afraid. Lord Poole had not seen her speaking to Mr. Lowell, she was sure of it, but the thought he *might* have done so kept her lying awake for hours. The threats he had made hung over her head, taking some of the delight from her kiss with Mr. Lowell. She knew very well what he was offering her, knew he was giving her not only the chance to escape but also the opportunity to continue to explore the clear regard and affection that was growing between herself and Mr. Lowell, but the fear of what would come crashing down onto Lord and Lady Rutledge's head should she do so lingered like a malevolent shadow.

"I think we should take a carriage ride."

Georgiana lifted her head and looked at Lord Poole in surprise.

"The afternoon is cold but clear," he said, practically ordering her to obey. "How long will it take you to change?"

Georgiana looked down at her gown, realizing it was not a particularly warm one given she had not expected to be going out of doors this afternoon. "I should be ready within half an hour," she said, getting out of her chair quickly and feeling her stomach tying itself in knots. "If you would not mind waiting?"

He waved a hand. "Do ensure you have a maid with you also," he said firmly. "This is the last day I shall be in London. I return to my estate tomorrow. We have some matters to discuss as regards our wedding."

Georgiana, who did not understand why they could not discuss such things in the warmth and comfort of Lord Allerton's drawing-room, bobbed a quick curtsy and hurried from the room. Her stomach was twisting this way and that, her mind befuddled with so many thoughts and feelings that when she rounded a corner, she practically walked straight into Lady Allerton.

"Goodness, Georgiana!" Lady Allerton exclaimed as Georgiana stumbled back, apologizing. "Where are you going in such a hurry?" Her eyes fixed upon Georgiana's, a narrowing of her eyes telling Georgiana that her sister-in-law was not about to let her go past without a simple word of explanation. "I thought Lord Poole was present."

"He is waiting for me," Georgiana said quickly, making to walk past her sister-in-law. "We are to take a carriage ride."

Lady Allerton frowned, turned, and began to accompany Georgiana up the staircase. "But you were to have him for afternoon tea."

"And now he wants to take a carriage ride," Georgiana said with a shrug. "So, therefore, I must change."

Lady Allerton sighed heavily but said nothing more until Georgiana had reached her bedchamber. As the maid came scurrying in after them both, Lady Allerton closed the door firmly, leaned against it, and fixed Georgiana with a firm gaze.

"Why are you obeying whatever Lord Poole asks of

you, Georgiana?" she asked, her voice almost accusing in its tone. "He says you are to go for a carriage ride, and you immediately go to change instead of stating the agreement was to take tea."

Georgiana swallowed hard, looking back at Lady Allerton and wondering if she ought to tell her the truth. "I—I am merely trying to please my betrothed," she answered lamely, knowing that such words were nothing more than falsehood. "Is that not the right thing to do?" She stepped to one side as the maid began to undo the buttons on the back of her gown.

"No, it is not," Lady Allerton answered with a firmness that surprised Georgiana. "You might well wish to do as he asks, but only if that comes from a place of regard, of affection." She took a few steps further into the room but did not lift her eyes from Georgiana's face. "But if you are doing it out of fear, then that is quite wrong."

Georgiana closed her eyes but said nothing, feeling a swell of emotion rise up within her, threatening to break over her.

"Ever since you returned from your walk with Lord Poole some days ago, you have retreated into a shell that none of us can break apart," Lady Allerton said softly, coming closer to Georgiana as Georgiana opened her eyes. "What is it he has said that makes you so afraid?"

Georgiana closed her eyes again and shook her head mutely. There had been so much happening these last few days she could barely keep her thoughts in coherent order. Last evening, she had given into the desires of her heart and had kissed Mr. Lowell with all the passion she felt. It had been only momentary, but it felt as though she had lingered there for much longer. She knew very well what Mr. Lowell was offering her, what he was asking of her, but there was still a great fear within her heart. A fear that, should she accept him, Mr. Lowell might then be brought to ruin, that Lord and Lady Rutledge would have pain and scandal brought to their door by her actions.

You could go to America with him.

A small shiver ran down her spine at the thought. That was what Mr. Lowell had been offering her, had been asking of her, but Georgiana had thrown that idea aside almost at once. She could not even *think* of going to America with him, not when she would have to cry off from her engagement, and that in itself would bring scandal. A scandal that would, inevitably, touch Lord and Lady Allerton also. On top of which, Georgiana was quite sure that Lord Poole would do all he could to ruin Mr. Lowell's good name, and in doing so, bring shame to Lord and Lady Rutledge, just as he had threatened.

"What is it, Georgiana?"

Lady Allerton's voice was soft and filled with compassion and concern. Georgiana shook her head and stepped into a warmer gown, the deep red suiting her coloring very well indeed.

"There is something wrong," Lady Allerton said softly, putting one hand on Georgiana's arm. "Why will you not tell me what it is? I might be able to help." Her eyes searched Georgiana's face. "I know you are afraid of Lord Poole. You should talk to your brother about whatever it is Lord Poole has done to upset you. The match might not be suitable after all."

"But it is agreed!" Georgiana exclaimed, the sound of her voice filling the room and startling not only the maid but also Lady Allerton herself. "The agreement is done. I am to marry Lord Poole, and there is nothing that can prevent that."

Lady Allerton blinked in surprise and, with a wave of her hand, dismissed the maid. "What do you mean, my dear?" she asked as the maid hurried to the door. "You know very well you can cry off."

Georgiana shook her head. "The scandal," she said hopelessly, dropping her head. "And there is no promise that I should find someone else to marry me."

Lady Allerton's brow lifted. "Not even Mr. Lowell?" she asked gently. "I know he cares for you and you care for him." A small smile lifted her mouth as Georgiana looked up sharply. "You do not need to pretend, my dear. I know what it is like to have a deep affection for another. I can see it in your eyes and in the way he looks at you." Tenderly, she smiled to herself. "Lord Allerton has the very same look in his gaze when he looks at me."

Georgiana wanted to break down into tears, her emotions held just below the surface and no more. Her pain was growing steadily, her confusion mounting, and yet Lady Allerton's words spoke the truth to her heart.

"He has offered to take me to America," she whispered brokenly. "But Lord Poole has threatened to ruin Mr. Lowell and spread the scandal to his cousin and her husband, should I go near to him again."

There was a long pause and, when Georgiana looked up, she saw nothing but anger in her sister-in-law's eyes.

"He is threatening you?" she asked hoarsely, her eyes

now burning with an inner fire that Georgiana could almost feel. "Lord Poole?"

Without even realizing she was doing it, Georgiana put a hand to her cheek, remembering how Lord Poole had struck her. She had managed to hide it from both her brother and sister-in-law, but the fear and the upset she felt had gone deep into her soul. Lady Allerton narrowed her eyes all the more, stepping forward so she was closer to Georgiana now.

"Georgiana," she said firmly, looking at Georgiana square in the face. "If your brother knew that Lord Poole had done anything to hurt you, then he would not hesitate to bring an end to your engagement."

Georgiana closed her eyes tightly, feeling hot tears prick at the corners of her eyes. "I did not want to upset you, Alice," she said, her voice breaking with the emotion that swamped her. "But I am so very confused. I should be grateful that my brother has found me a decent match. Lord Poole is...titled and wealthy and refined, even if he lacks the excellent character I had hoped for." Sniffing, she opened her eyes, glad that no tears fell to her cheeks. "It is foolish to consider Mr. Lowell," she finished brokenly. "If I leave a trail of scandal and lies behind me, which will not only affect Mr. Lowell but also his cousin, then I should never forgive myself."

Lady Allerton closed her eyes and let out a long breath, her knuckles white as she grasped the back of a chair. It was clear to Georgiana she was trying her best to keep her temper, making Georgiana fear that her sister-in-law might do something unexpected and entirely unwise.

"I should marry Lord Poole, as I am expected to do," Georgiana whispered in the hope that this would make things better. "He is right to say that I ought not to become too close to Mr. Lowell."

"No." Lady Allerton opened her eyes and looked at Georgiana directly, her expression set. "No, Georgiana, that is precisely what you ought *not* to do." She gave her a small smile. "You should not give in to blackmail or threats. That is not the sort of gentleman we thought Lord Poole to be." Her eyes dropped to the floor for a moment, an expression of regret rippling across her face. "Quiet, refined, and perhaps a little cool in his character, but never cruel." Lifting her gaze back to Georgiana, she shook her head. "I will speak to Allerton."

Georgiana swallowed hard, fear beginning to bite at her again. "But what if something is done that will bring about what Lord Poole has threatened?"

Lady Allerton hesitated, clearly unable to give Georgiana an answer that would satisfy her. "I—I do not know," she said honestly. "But I must hope that your brother will think of a way to let you free of this engagement without there being any particularly grave consequences." Her head tilted just a little, a question in her eyes. "And when you are free, Georgiana, what then?"

The question hung in the air between them, and Georgiana caught her breath, feeling butterflies begin to stir in the pit of her belly.

"Mr. Lowell will be returning to America soon after Christmas," Lady Allerton reminded her, gently. "The time to speak to him of what you feel is at hand."

Georgiana shook her head, pressing her hands to her

eyes for a moment. "I—I need to think," she said eventually. "I have been very lost and confused these last few days. When I was dancing with Mr. Lowell last evening, I..." She trailed off, the moment coming back to her with all swiftness. She had felt safe in his arms, had felt as though this was the right place for her to be. It had been only a moment, but it had meant so much to her, she did not think she would be able to forget it for the rest of her life.

"I will not pretend that leaving one's home to start a new life somewhere new is not difficult," Lady Allerton said softly, stepping forward and taking Georgiana's hand. "I know exactly how it feels. But, and I can assure you of this, if you are loved by another, if you are held tightly in their heart, then the pain and the sorrow of leaving behind one's home becomes less. It grows less and less each day until you find yourself quite content."

Georgiana nodded, tears beginning to creep down her cheeks. "I do feel afraid of what will happen if I give full sway to my feelings," she said honestly. "It would mean leaving everything behind, but the thought of saying goodbye to Mr. Lowell, never to see him again, is almost more than I can bear."

Lady Allerton nodded sagely, clearly understanding everything Georgiana had expressed. "Then take your walk with Lord Poole," she said, pressing Georgiana's hands. "Do not say a word to him about what we have discussed. Rather, continue as normal. When you return, your brother and I will have talked about what you have told me, and, together, I am sure we can come up with something." She smiled warmly. "Whether or not you *do* decide to tell Mr. Lowell the truth of your heart or allow him to return to America without ever expressing it, I do not think any longer that Lord Poole is the right gentleman for you, Georgiana. I do wish you had spoken to me earlier of your struggle."

Georgiana could not speak, such was the lump in her throat. All she could do was press her sister-in-law's hands tightly, wanting her to know just how grateful she was.

"Then I will let you finish preparing," Lady Allerton said gently. "And we will speak at length when you return."

"The wedding is to take place a week after Christmas."

Georgiana looked up at her betrothed, realizing just how timid she was before him. She had not always been this way, she noted, aware that when they had first met, she had been very dismissive of him. It had been ever since he had struck her, ever since he had made those dark and devious threats, that she had retreated inside herself until she was almost too afraid to move. Her sister-in-law was clearly angry with Lord Poole's actions, whereas she was still quite afraid.

That awareness did not bring her any joy. Rather, it made her feel almost sick with frustration and upset. This was not the sort of young lady she wished to be! She wanted to be confident, secure, and happy—and such things would not be discovered if she remained in Lord Poole's company!

"Did you hear me, Lady Georgiana?"

Lord Poole's voice was harsh and angry, making her jerk her head up.

"I did," she replied, trying to keep the tremor from her voice and looking deep within herself for the courage she knew she would soon need. "A week after Christmas."

"I am to return to my estate tomorrow, now that the roads are *finally* clear enough for my carriage," he continued, looking at her with a dark expression. "You will send word to me the moment you have returned to your brother's estate, which I presume will be very soon."

Georgiana blinked, then lifted one shoulder in a small shrug. "I will have to ask my brother."

"There is no reason for you to remain in London," Lord Poole said, his tone accusing. "Unless there is something you have not yet told me?"

Her chest tightened, but Georgiana forced herself to look up into Lord Poole's face as they drew near to his carriage. "I do not know what you mean, Lord Poole," she said with as much coldness in her tone as she could muster. "Shall we return? It is very cold." Snow had not been falling for a few days now, but the cold and the chill meant the ground was still frozen hard, and Georgiana could feel the wind whipping through her skirts, making her shiver. "And I know my brother will want me to return swiftly, given our walk was unplanned."

Lord Poole stopped right in front of the carriage, turning around to look at Georgiana so that his gaze was fixed on hers. His expression was dark, his eyes angry, and his face almost bloodless with the cold.

"You do not think I am a fool, I hope."

Georgiana swallowed but kept her expression blank. "I do not," she answered honestly.

"Then you must know that I am aware you have a closeness with Mr. Lowell you simply *refuse* to set aside," he said angrily. "I may not have been present in the ballroom last evening, Lady Georgiana, but I have acquaintances who *were* present and who saw you there with him." His eyes narrowed all the more. "I did warn you, Lady Georgiana."

Georgiana felt herself tremble but held her frame steady. Looking up into her betrothed eyes, she tried to find the strength to stand up to him, to tell him she was not afraid of his threats when the truth of it was, she was afraid of the consequences that would follow.

"There is no reason for me to give up any acquaintance with Mr. Lowell just because you demand it," she said, aware her voice was shaking but forcing herself to remain as calm as she could. "I am not the sort of young lady that will be pushed to one direction and then the other by way of your demands."

His lip curled. "You and I are betrothed, Lady Georgiana," he hissed, leaning down over her. "Or do you forget that we are soon to be wed?"

"And what if I do not wish it?" she asked, her heart in her throat as she tried her best to speak with strength. "What if I have decided that we will not suit?"

Silence grew between them like a dark cloud, but Georgiana held her gaze with every fiber of her being. Her courage grew slowly, but the memory of being in Mr. Lowell's arms helped her all the more. *He* was the man she ought to be considering, not Lord Poole. A title meant nothing; wealth lost its sheen in the face of a disagreeable, if not downright cruel nature.

"You dare to suggest you would cry off?" Lord Poole demanded, seeming to grow in size in front of her, seeming to fill every inch of her vision. "You dare even to *think* you would bring that sort of shame to me?"

Georgiana opened her mouth to speak, only for something to slam hard against the side of her head. She staggered to one side, her eyes squeezed shut with the pain of it. She could hear Lord Poole continuing to rail at her, could hear his angry voice and his furious exclamations, but they all seemed to be coming from very far away. In fact, she could hear very little, she realized, as the darkness began to clutch at her, pulling her in towards itself until she could hear nothing at all.

CHAPTER TEN

"You have a note, Lowell."

Oliver looked up with interest as Lady Rutledge handed him a note that had evidently just arrived. He had been making arrangements for his return to America, having decided to linger until after Christmas as he had first intended, but there was now another question in his mind. Ought he to book passage for only himself or for himself and a companion? A companion whom he hoped would be Lady Georgiana.

"Thank you," he murmured, turning the note over and seeing the wax seal there. Not quite certain who it belonged to, be broke the wax quickly and opened up the note.

A stifled gasp came from his mouth as he read the words over and over again, hardly able to take in the dreadful news. Even as he read the words, he felt his heart begin to pound furiously with a deep and fearful dread that swept all through him, right into his very bones.

"Goodness, Lowell!" Lady Rutledge exclaimed as he set the note on the table and stared at her in horror. "Whatever is the matter?"

Oliver blew out a long breath and shook his head. "I must go to her at once."

"Go to whom?" Lady Rutledge insisted, now looking quite alarmed. "What is wrong, Lowell?"

Staring at his cousin as though he could not quite see her, Oliver let out a long breath and tried to compose himself. "It is Lady Georgiana," he told her, his voice a little hoarse. "She went for a short carriage ride with Lord Poole yesterday afternoon and..." He saw his cousin's eyebrows lifting and knew precisely what she was thinking. "She has not returned. I know you will think she has eloped or some such thing, but there was no reason for her to do that. She and Lord Poole were already engaged."

Lady Rutledge frowned. "She cannot have gone too far," she said cautiously. "The snow has been falling overnight, and now the streets are almost impassible with the sheer amount of it." Gesturing to the window, she watched Oliver with interest. "But why should such a thing concern you? Lady Georgiana was an acquaintance only."

Oliver shook his head, rising from his chair. "I care for Lady Georgiana," he said bluntly, as Lady Rutledge's eyes flared wide. "I have offered to marry her and to take her back to Boston with me, but she is afraid."

"Afraid of what?" Lady Rutledge asked, looking a little pleased at Oliver's announcement. "Afraid of beginning her life all over again in America? That is something I can well understand."

Shaking his head again, Oliver began to pace up and down the room, his hand at his chin. "She never mentioned that, although I would expect there to be *some* trepidation. No, she was afraid of...Lord Poole." His eyes flicked towards Lady Rutledge, who now looked upset. "Her betrothed, I believe, had threatened her. Threatened to spread rumors and the like about both myself and you or Lord Rutledge, should she be seen in my company."

"But that is monstrous!" Lady Rutledge exclaimed, clearly horrified. "Why should he demand such a thing as that?"

Oliver did not immediately answer, leaving Lady Rutledge to come to her own conclusions. Sighing, he rubbed one hand down his face, coming to a stop and looking at his cousin with a furrowed brow.

"I must go to Lady Allerton," he said quietly. "I must go and speak to her. Surely there is something that can be done in order to find and protect Lady Georgiana."

Lady Rutledge, who had gone a little pale, nodded fervently but said nothing. Oliver wisely went to ring the bell for tea, fearing the shock of hearing such a threat might overcome her.

"You will not mind if I take my leave now?" he asked a little quietly. "Lord Rutledge is at home, is he not?"

Lady Rutledge gave herself a slight shake, looking up at Oliver with a determined expression. "Yes, yes he is," she said with a good deal more force than before. "And you must not worry about me. The threat of rumors is not something that I shall shy away from."

"But they could do you a great deal of harm," Oliver answered gravely. "Surely you must know that."

"I do," Lady Rutledge answered firmly, "but I will not allow *anyone* to blackmail either you or Lady Georgiana in such a terrible manner. How odious a gentleman Lord Poole must be!"

Oliver, who had been thinking the same thing for quite some time, could only agree. He pressed his cousin's shoulder for a moment and then hurried from the room. He had only one intention now. Find Lady Georgiana before it was too late.

"Thank you for coming, Mr. Lowell."

Lady Allerton grasped Oliver's hands the moment he came into the room. Lord Allerton rose and immediately handed Oliver a brandy, his face quite pinched.

"At once, of course," Oliver replied firmly, searching Lady Allerton's face. "I presume Lady Georgiana has not been found?"

Lady Allerton shook her head and glanced hopelessly back at her husband.

"We do not know where she or Lord Poole are gone," Lord Allerton grated. "Lady Allerton spoke to me of what had gone between herself and Georgiana before Georgiana went out with Lord Poole. I believe Lord Poole knew that Lady Georgiana would, at some point, seek to break off her engagement, although she had not come to such a decision herself at that time."

Something like hope fired straight through Oliver's soul. "She wanted to bring things to an end?" he asked as Lady Allerton nodded. "I am glad to hear it."

"I believe she had discovered happiness with someone other than Lord Poole," Lady Allerton answered softly, looking at him with a direct gaze. "But she was afraid of the consequences."

Oliver sank into a chair, his stomach knotting. "The threats."

"Indeed," Lord Allerton muttered, looking sorrow-fully towards his wife as if seeking her forgiveness. "I confess, I thought I had done well in choosing Lord Poole for my sister. From what I knew of him, he was quiet and reserved, but I never once thought him so...sinister."

"It is not your fault, Allerton," his wife murmured whilst Oliver nodded fervently in agreement. "All we need to concentrate on is finding Georgiana."

Lord Allerton nodded, his jaw tightening as a vein began to throb in his forehead. "There will be a scandal," he said hoarsely. "Whatever will we do?"

Lady Allerton glanced towards Oliver, a knowing look in her eyes—and it was all Oliver could do not to speak. She gave him the tiniest of smiles before pressing her husband's arm.

"It will be quite all right, my dear," she whispered as Lord Allerton closed his eyes in evident frustration. "I am quite sure it will work out for the best. There may not even *be* a scandal if we find her quickly enough."

Oliver took a small step forward. "I know that rumors

can spread quickly," he said, well aware of how difficult London society could be. "But no one aside from the three of us and my cousin know she is gone."

"We will not be able to hide it for long," Lord Allerton muttered. "Georgiana's maid is aware of her absence, but I have absolute certainty she will keep such a thing to herself." He grimaced, making Oliver wonder what it was Lord Allerton had said to have such an assurance. "I do not even know where to begin to look."

Oliver rubbed at his forehead, frowning hard. "Lord Poole's residence?" he suggested as Lord Allerton shook his head. "You have looked there already."

"I called earlier," Lord Allerton said with a heavy sigh. "Lord Poole has gone back to his estate."

"But he cannot have done so," Oliver said at once, confused. "The snow has fallen heavily overnight, and my cousin has said that—"

"You are quite right," Lady Allerton said interrupting him. "We do not believe he has left London. Although why he has taken Georgiana, I cannot imagine. Why not let her cry off? Why not accept the match would not work?"

"Because," Oliver said grimly, recalling how upset Lady Georgiana had been and knowing how afraid she had become of the gentleman, "because he is a man used to getting what he desires. He would not accept the shame or the embarrassment of her crying off, so the only way to prevent it—"

"Is to force her into wedlock."

Lord Allerton went very pale indeed, and for a moment, Oliver thought he might stumble forward in shock. His own stomach twisted hard, feeling sick at the thought of what might happen to Lady Georgiana at the hand of Lord Poole.

"We must find her," Lady Allerton said, sounding all the more desperate. "But where are we to look?"

Oliver shook his head to himself, trying his best to think of what to suggest. Try as he might, he could think of nowhere to begin. He did not know London well enough to think of where Lord Poole might have taken her.

"Did she ever say anything to you, Alice?" he heard Lord Allerton say, speaking directly to his wife. "Did she ever mention somewhere that Lord Poole had taken her to, or wished to take her to visit?"

Oliver's head snapped up, his whole being jolted with a sudden shock. "I do remember something," he said hurriedly, looking at Lord Allerton. "It might well be nothing of consequence, but Lady Georgiana did tell me that Lord Poole has a brother here in London."

There was a second or two of silence before both Lord Allerton and Lady Allerton began to speak. Their questions were much the same, however, and Oliver was able to answer them both.

"Lady Georgiana did not tell me the name of this brother, no," he said a little frustrated. "Perhaps she didn't know. All I can remember is she said Lord Poole's brother resided in London also."

Lord Allerton bit his lip and looked to his wife. "We must discover him," he said as Lady Allerton nodded quickly, her hands now grasping those of her husband. "If Georgiana is not there, then this brother might well provide an answer as to the whereabouts of Lord Poole."

Despite having remembered something that could now provide at least the beginnings of an answer as to Lady Georgiana's whereabouts, Oliver felt useless. He did not know what he should do or where he should go, looking from one to the other expectantly.

"I will go to call upon Lady Winters," Lady Allerton was saying. "She may well know who this gentleman is."

"And I will go to Whites," Lord Allerton said with a nod. "Someone surely must know something." Wincing, he looked at Oliver. "Although given I did not know the man's true character, I wonder if I ever really knew him at all."

Trying to smile in sympathy, Oliver lifted one shoulder in a half-shrug. "And what shall I do?" he asked, spreading his hands. "I don't know London very well, and I certainly have very little idea as to who to ask, but I should like to do something."

Lord Allerton glanced at his wife, a look of uncertainty in his eyes.

"Might you wait here?" Lady Allerton suggested, looking back at him with a sudden sharpness in her gaze. "If Lord Poole should send word—or if something should occur—it would be best if someone was here."

"I could not ask you to go to Whites in my place, for example," Lord Allerton added with a slightly rueful smile. "And Lady Allerton could not bring you to Lady Winters."

Oliver nodded, trying to get rid of the feeling he was being more than useless. "Of course," he agreed, wishing there was something more to do. "I would be glad to wait."

"And I shall have the butler bring you any correspondence," Lady Allerton finished, already making for the door. "Just in case it is from Lord Poole."

"Thank you," Oliver answered as Lord Allerton followed after his wife. "I will wait here for your return and pray you have found some answer."

There came no reply for, as his words floated across the room, Lord Allerton shut the door tightly behind him, leaving Oliver standing entirely alone, feeling more inadequate than ever before.

"Nothing?"

Oliver stared at Lord Allerton and then turned his gaze to Lady Allerton, who was wearing the same look of misery as her husband. They had been gone for at least two hours, and he had done nothing but pace up and down the room and drink a little of Lord Allerton's excellent French brandy. All the while, he had silently prayed that Lady Georgiana was quite safe, she was unharmed, and that Lord and Lady Allerton would find success in their ventures. Surely God would be looking down on them, especially at this time of year, he had thought, whilst knowing full well that such a thought was nothing more than foolishness.

And now, his heart felt as though it had been ripped from his chest and flung down to the floor, leaving nothing but a gaping hole in its place. Whilst they had been gone, Oliver had kept that faint hope alive, had been praying there would be something found that would bring them an answer, bring them something to go on—but to hear that there was nothing of use at all made him both upset and frustrated.

It seemed as though Lady Georgiana was to remain lost in the ether of London.

"Lady Winters knew nothing of Lord Poole," Lady Allerton said, slumped in a chair as she gazed, unseeingly, at the fire that burned in the grate. "She knew his name, of course, but knew nothing of his family or anything of particular interest."

"And neither did any gentleman I spoke to in Whites," Lord Allerton muttered, looking entirely wretched. "There was not even the suggestion made as to who else I might think of asking!" Groaning aloud, he sat forward with his hands on his knees, raking his hands through his hair. "She is lost."

Closing his eyes tightly, Oliver let out a long, slow breath, telling himself not to panic and certainly not to give way to fear. One thing was for certain—he would not even *think* about returning to America without first ensuring that Lady Georgiana was quite safe.

"Then surely the only thing we can do," he began, slowly, his mind trying to find some answer to what was a seemingly impossible situation, "is to sit outside Lord Poole's townhouse and watch for any comings and goings that might be out of the ordinary."

Lord Allerton lifted his head, but no light shone in his eyes.

"There is nothing else we can do," Oliver continued

with a small shrug. "It is the only thing I can think of that might bring us even the smallest hope."

Lady Allerton began to nod slowly, her eyes turning from Oliver to her husband. "Mr. Lowell is right," she said quietly, her voice holding nothing but grief. "We must act, Allerton!"

Very slowly, Lord Allerton began to nod, beginning to unfold himself from his chair and looking up at Oliver. "And if we find nothing?"

Refusing to allow himself even to *think* about such a thing, Oliver shook his head. "We must hope that we find or see something," he answered, knowing that to dwell on what he might not see would only bring his spirits lower. "I will go, of course. You are both exhausted and need to rest." He heard both Lord and Lady Allerton begin to protest but held up his hands in quiet sternness. "I insist," he said a little more loudly as he looked Lady Allerton in the eye. "You have both had quite enough for the time being; I can see it in both your faces. Rest, eat, and try to sleep if you can. I will return the moment I see anything."

Lord Allerton let out a long, slow breath, but his expression grew firm. "No," he answered decisively. "I will not let you sit out there alone. You may go first, Mr. Lowell, but once my wife and I have rested and eaten, we will join you." He gave a small smile to his wife, who held his gaze. "I know that I could not sleep even if I tried."

"Nor I," Lady Allerton replied, looking towards Oliver. "You are being very kind, Mr. Lowell, and I know it is because you care for Georgiana. My gratitude is more than I can express." She pressed one hand lightly to her forehead. "But you are right. I will need to rest for a time and mayhap..." A glance was sent towards her husband. "Mayhap you might join Mr. Lowell, Allerton. If there was to come a note or a messenger to the house and no one was here to receive it, then I would never forgive myself."

Oliver swallowed a sudden ache in his throat, pushing away the fears that by the time he saw Lady Georgiana again, she would be so far from his reach, he might never have the chance to tell her the true depths of his affection. "I am sure we will find her," he said with a confidence he did not quite feel. "Rest, Lady Allerton. And pray, for that is all I think we can do."

Some hours later and Oliver felt as though his feet had turned to blocks of ice. The blankets wrapped around him had been a warm comfort to him within the first few hours, but as the night began to take a hold of London, the cold had wrapped around his bones.

The hackney they had taken had done nothing other than sit a short distance away from Lord Poole's town-house. This part of London was rather busy, even this late at night, so no one would think anything of it—but both Oliver and then Lord Allerton's eyes had been fixed solely on the front door that led to Lord Poole's home. A footman, dressed in somewhat shabby clothes for the sole purpose of sneaking around to the servant's entrance, had also been gone for some hours, meaning there was nothing of note to yet report.

And with each minute that passed, Oliver felt his spirits sinking lower.

Lord Poole had taken Lady Georgiana away somewhere, he was sure of it, simply so she would not be able to cry off and so he would not have to bear the shame or disgrace that came thereafter. What she wanted and what she needed were of little importance to him, it seemed. All he cared for was his contentment, and he did not care what he inflicted on others to get it.

Oliver could not imagine how Lord Allerton was feeling. He had expressed, on more than one occasion, just how wrong he had been about Lord Poole's character, and Oliver had been required to reassure him that this was not his doing. But he could practically see Lord Allerton sinking lower and lower in spirit with every minute that passed.

"I do not know what I will do," Lord Allerton muttered, clearly upset now. "When she returns home— for I must believe she will be returned—if she is unwed, then what shall I do?" His eyes lifted to Oliver's face, his features shrouded in shadows, illuminated only by the flickering light from the lantern that hung on one side of the hackney. "She will not be sought out by any gentleman then, not when this has occurred."

"The *ton* might not even know about this," Oliver responded as reassuringly as he could. "If we find her soon, then the staff will say nothing, and her reputation will be protected."

Lord Allerton shook his head. "She always wanted to find her own suitor," he mumbled, although Oliver could not tell if this was something Lord Allerton agreed with or found rather foolish. "She did as I asked her, of course, and knew my reasons for doing so, but that idea never went away."

Something began to stir in Oliver's heart, something that made him look away from Lord Allerton, his eyes turning back towards Lord Poole's townhouse.

"Perhaps she would have had a better success of things if I'd allowed her to do that," Lord Allerton continued, almost mournfully. "There were not a great many gentlemen willing to court her, of course, and in fact, she had not had a single one come to seek her out, but I still wonder if..." He trailed off, leaving Oliver to fill the silence.

"I am sure that whatever you chose to do was for Lady Georgiana's best," he said, his heart beginning to quicken as he kept his hopes hidden away. What if Lord Allerton told Lady Georgiana she could choose her suitor? If he were to propose to Lady Georgiana then, knowing she had that freedom, would she accept him? He was certain there was something of an affection in Lady Georgiana's heart for him, but just how deep it went, Oliver could not say.

"Wait."

Something caught his eye—a flash of something, nothing more. Oliver leaned forward, his eyes fixed on Lord Poole's townhouse, his hands curling into fists as though he expected someone to leap out and plant him a facer.

"My lord!"

A sudden gasping exclamation had both gentlemen jumping visibly in their seats, turning to see Lord Allerton's footman standing at one side of the hackney, his face pressed to the window.

"Good gracious, man!" Lord Allerton exclaimed as the footman pulled the door and made to continue speaking, only for Lord Allerton to half pull him, half help him inside, the door closed again behind him. "What is it?"

"I did not want to say until I was sure," the footman said shivering violently with the cold. "But the very same servant has come back to the house three times."

"Come back?" Oliver repeated, a little confused. "What do you mean?"

The footman shivered again, and Lord Allerton pulled a blanket from his knees and handed it to his servant, who practically grabbed it from his master and flung it around his shoulders. The man was half frozen with cold.

"A servant of some description has come into the house through the servant's entrance, and then has left again shortly afterward," he explained, glancing at Oliver. "He always has something to take with him, although I do not know what it can be."

Lord Allerton nodded grimly, shooting a look at Oliver, who himself nodded in agreement. This was something they could explore, at least, something they might look into.

"And you say this servant has come and gone three times?"

The footman nodded. "Almost every hour," he said, his shivering now a little less violent than before. "He has only just come back."

Lord Allerton's eyes widened. "You mean to say, this servant has come back to the house for a fourth time?"

"And if I am right," the servant said quickly, "he will leave again soon. You must watch carefully, my lord. It is easy enough to miss him."

"You have done very well," Lord Allerton murmured as the servant inclined his head. "I will not ask you to step outside again." He gave his servant a half-smile. "Here." Pulling out a few coins from his pocket, he handed them to the footman, who stared at them, wide-eyed. "Make sure you get a hackney back to the house and the rest, you may keep," Lord Allerton told him. "And pray tell Lady Allerton what you have told us. She will want to know."

The servant began to stammer his thanks, promising he would do everything Lord Allerton had asked of him before exiting the hackney, leaving Oliver to stare fixedly out of the window.

"You do know he might keep all of that and merely walk home," he murmured as Lord Allerton moved to sit next to him, so he too might stare out of the window in the direction of Lord Poole's townhouse. "At least, that is the sort of thing I would do."

Lord Allerton chuckled, seemingly now pulled from his doldrums and filled with a new hope. "I do not mind what he does," he answered as Oliver narrowed his eyes to get a better view. "The boy has done well."

"Very well," Oliver replied, his voice lowering as though he were afraid they might be overheard somehow. "Let's hope that this leads us somewhere."

Silence filled the hackney for a few minutes. Oliver could feel his tension rising, could feel his frustration begin to fill his heart as they continued to wait. He had to pray that the footman had seen something of importance, something that would lead them to find Lady Georgiana. His heart ached for her, his mind praying silently she was safe.

"There!"

Lord Allerton pointed with one long finger, leaving Oliver to strain his eyes to see who was being pointed out. Finally, he saw him. A short, thin fellow, dressed in a coat of gray that seemed to match the snow and the mud that lined the streets, had begun to scurry along the cobbled pathway, not looking to the right or the left but straight ahead of him.

"What will we do?" Oliver asked, his whole body rigid with the urge to act. "Follow him on foot?"

"No, I—" Lord Allerton was cut short as he saw the man climb into a waiting hackney, letting out a quiet exclamation. Wherever this man was going, it was clearly some distance away, *and* he had enough funds to pay for the trip.

"We need to follow that hackney," Oliver muttered as Lord Allerton rapped hard on the roof, shouting the very same thing to the driver.

"But carefully now!" Lord Allerton called out as the driver began to push his horses out onto the street. "Do not make our pursuit apparent! There will be an extra payment in this for you if you succeed."

This, Oliver was sure, would have the driver do everything that was expected of him, and, as the hackney pulled away, Oliver felt his tiny flickering hope begin to build into something stronger. Perhaps they would find

Lady Georgiana after all. Perhaps she would be quite safe, and perhaps, finally, she would be free of Lord Poole. That was all he wanted for her, all he hoped for her. To be free of the gentleman she had thought would be the right suitor, the right husband for her. To be free to make her own choices and her own decisions when it came to matters of the heart. That was all Oliver prayed for, knowing that a creature as lovely, as kind, and as considerate as Lady Georgiana deserved nothing but goodness in this world, nothing but joy and happiness. He only prayed she would soon find it.

CHAPTER ELEVEN

*I*t was very dark by the time Georgiana finally managed to open her eyes. For whatever reason, her eyelids felt very heavy indeed, and there was a slight pain to the side of her head.

"What happened?" she said aloud, expecting Lady Allerton or her brother to answer her—but there came no reply. Blinking rapidly, Georgiana felt a clutching hand of fear grasp at her heart, making her breath catch. Looking all about her, she finally saw a small sliver of light coming from one end of whatever room she was in. Had her sister-in-law put her to bed for some reason? Had she become ill? Unable to recall anything that had happened, Georgiana slowly sat up, her feet swinging down onto the cold floor.

She shivered. The room was very cold indeed, with no fire in the grate and no warmth coming from any other part of the room. It was very odd for the maids not to have lit a fire in her room, especially when they knew it had become so very cold of late. Frowning, Georgiana rubbed her arms with her hands, realizing she was still wearing her gown and not her night things. She stopped dead, her feet still encased in her boots—and felt her heart begin to thud in a furious, panicked rhythm.

What had happened to her?

Closing her eyes, Georgiana let out a long, slow breath and tried to keep herself calm. Why could she not recall what had happened? Gingerly, she reached up and pressed the side of her head, wincing as pain shot through her temples. Had she injured herself?

"I will not panic," she said aloud as though it would help her contain her fears. "I will not give way to it." Settling her hands by her sides, she made her way to the chink of dull, gray light that was coming in through what she presumed were the windows. With no candle to speak of, Georgiana took each step slowly and carefully, afraid she might trip over something and end up hurting herself again—but the floor appeared to be quite empty. Her fingers reached out and touched a heavy curtain and, in one swift motion, she pulled it back and let her eyes adjust to the dull, gloomy scene before her.

"Where am I?"

Snow had fallen heavily, it seemed, for everything about her was bathed in white. The road had been cleared, although as more flakes of snow continued to fall, Georgiana thought that, very soon, it would be covered over completely. No one was walking through the streets at the present time, which did not surprise her given the lateness of the hour. The sky itself was a very dark gray, lit only by the flickering lanterns that lit the streets.

And then, Georgiana began to panic.

She had no idea where she was. There was nothing around her or in the street she recognized. This very house was not her brother's; this room was not her own. She had been taken somewhere she did not know, although she could not remember what had happened to make her obedient to such a scheme. It would not be Allerton himself who had done this, she was quite sure, which meant it might only be...

"Lord Poole."

Georgiana felt herself falling backward with the shock of what she had recalled, feeling herself hit the floor hard but feeling no pain. She was numb with fright, cold all over as she remembered what had happened.

Lord Poole had known she had kissed Mr. Lowell, had known she had been thinking of crying off. And then, something hard had struck her on the side of the head, and she had found herself falling into darkness.

Darkness which now bound her still. There was no easy escape from this particular prison. Without a light, she could not tell where she was nor how she was to get out. The chill caught her bones, and she shivered violently, her eyes staring, unseeingly, out at the window before her. Was she already married? Had Lord Poole found a way for her to give her consent without any words coming from her mouth? Shuddering again, Georgiana closed her eyes tightly, pulled her knees up to her chest, and rested her head on them for a few minutes, curling up as tight as she could manage. She felt very afraid, very fearful that Lord Poole would throw himself into the room and demand she give him what was expected of a wife.

The very thought made her sick with fear.

Closing her eyes tightly, Georgiana tried her best to force her fear down her throat and back into the depths of herself. She could not let it take hold, she told herself emphatically, screwing up her eyes and trying to find courage. Had she not already tried to be strong in front of Lord Poole? Had she not managed to tell him that yes, she had thought of crying off?

"And look where that has brought me," she whispered, a single tear tracking down her cheek as she opened her eyes and looked up into the darkness as though God himself might come down and bring her a little light. Nothing happened. The whole house remained silent, without even a single creak of a floorboard to indicate that anyone else was at home.

Christmas this year might very well turn out to be the most terrible one she had ever experienced. Tears began to fall in earnest as Georgiana sobbed, fear taking hold of her as racking sobs shook her frame. She did not know what to do and that scared her the most.

You have not tried the door.

The thought slammed hard into her mind, bringing her sobs to a sudden, complete stop. She had not even *thought* to go in search of the door, had only collapsed back onto the floor in shock. Gritting her teeth, Georgiana dashed her tears away in an attempt to grasp any kind of strength. She had to do something other than merely sit here and cry, she told herself. If Lord Poole was waiting below stairs, then did she not have the right to demand to know precisely what he was doing and what his intentions were? Could she not try her best to find a way to escape from this house and return home? Doubtfully, Georgiana bit her lip. She had very little idea as to where she was, and to rush out into the snow would be rather foolish...although perhaps to remain here would be all the more terrible.

A sudden sound caught her ears, making her catch her breath. The sound of muffled horses' hooves drew ever closer, and Georgiana forced herself to her feet, moving quietly towards the window and looking out at the snow-covered street.

A hackney had only just pulled up outside the house. As she watched, she saw a servant leap down from it, a package under his arm. Paying the driver, he made towards the house—only to look up and stare directly into Georgiana's face.

Georgiana stared back at him, horror-stricken and yet unable to look away. The man was older than she had expected, and, as she watched, she saw a smirk tug at the man's lips, his eyes glistening in the dim light before he lowered his head and carried on inside.

Georgiana wanted to break down and cry all over again, afraid of what she had seen in the man's face, afraid of what he might do or what he might tell Lord Poole, but she forced herself to drag in long breaths, forced herself to stand tall and to push the shaking from her limbs.

A memory of Mr. Lowell looking deeply into her eyes began to burn in her mind, sending a new wave of strength to her cold limbs. He had offered her something wonderful, something entirely new, and she had been too afraid even to allow herself to think about it. Mr. Lowell had stolen her heart, and she had been too scared to admit it to herself.

Lord Poole had made sure of that. He had used nothing more than threats, anger, and demands to force her to obey, to force her to do as he requested rather than permitting her to imagine a life entirely different from what had been set out for her. She had given in to it, had done all he had asked out of nothing more than fear. And he would continue to use that fear against her, Georgiana realized, pressing one hand lightly to the side of her head. Was she going to permit him to do that when she still had a chance to escape? If she told her brother the truth, then yes, there would be a scandal when it came to crying off, but Georgiana knew that her brother would much prefer that than to permit Georgiana to marry someone so cruel.

And what of Lord and Lady Rutledge? said a quiet voice in her head. *If you do this, then they could be covered with such a great scandal that they might never emerge. Their good name could be afflicted forever. Their children might never be able to lift their heads.*

"And whose doing would that be?" Georgiana said aloud, almost arguing with her thoughts. "That would not be my doing." She lifted her chin just a little, remembering the warmth in Mr. Lowell's eyes and comparing it to the cold arrogance she saw in Lord Poole. "I would not bring such scandal. That would be Lord Poole entirely." There was still abundant doubt in her heart, still a good measure of fear, but Georgiana did not want to let go of the courage she *had* found thus far. Lifting her chin, she took in another steadying breath, turning around to fumble her way across the room to find the door—only to see something more.

Another hackney.

Frowning, Georgiana looked out towards it and, much to her astonishment, saw first her brother and then Mr. Lowell stepping out of it. They looked at the houses in turn, an expression of confusion on their faces as they looked from one to the next. They were looking for her, she realized, as a surge of hope burned in her heart. Without realizing what she was doing, she began to wave frantically, one hand banging on the glass pane of the window to attract their attention.

It worked almost instantaneously. The two gentlemen looked up at her window at once, but neither of them smiled nor looked delighted to see her. Instead, they continued to frown, their eyes fixed on her window but without showing any sign of recognition.

They cannot see me, she realized, looking behind her into the dark room and realizing that in the gloom, all they might be able to see would be a flickering shadow. Shoving the heavy curtains a little further back, she began to wave again, one fist hammering on the window as the two gentlemen drew closer. If she only had a candle or some such thing, then they might be able to see her a little more clearly.

She watched as her brother said something to Mr. Lowell, who nodded, before turning his eyes back up to her window. Slumping just a little, she saw them both approach the house, disappearing from her view as they walked towards the door.

A new energy filled her as she heard the echoes of

their knock at the door. They were looking for her, and yet there was still the chance they might be turned away, might easily be refused entrance into the house by whatever servants worked here. Frantically, Georgiana hurried across the room, wincing as her foot hit the edge of the bed, sending another wave of pain up her spine. Shaking her head to herself, Georgiana moved closer to the other side of the room, her fingers held out in front of her as she tried to find the door handle.

She could hear nothing, could see nothing. There was no light anywhere, nothing but darkness surrounding her. Slowly, she made her way across the room, her fingers pushing along the wall with great care as she tried to find the door.

And then, something cold and smooth brushed her fingers.

The door handle.

Turning it quickly, Georgiana closed her eyes in frustration as the door remained unmoved. Lord Poole had locked it then, as she had expected. Biting her lip, Georgiana opened her eyes again and turned the door handle this way and that, shaking it, jiggling it, and doing all she could to try to have the door open.

Nothing seemed to work.

Her courage began to leave her as she fought the urge to sink to the floor, her head resting on the door itself for a few moments. Her fingers slipped from the door handle, her whole body now limp with a surge of hopelessness that tried to steal every part of her courage from her. She did not know what to do. The door was locked, and she did not think she would be able to remove herself from this place without the key.

"The master said we must not!"

A sudden whisper had Georgiana's ears pricking up, her body straightening, her head lifting from the door.

"I tell you, I heard something."

"That doesn't matter," came the first, louder voice. "The master said we were not to go near this room. It doesn't matter what's inside it."

"Please!"

Georgiana could not help but speak aloud, her heart clamoring furiously. "Please, might you let me out?"

There came nothing but silence for a long minute, leaving Georgiana fearful that the two voices—whoever they belonged to—had been chased away.

"I have done nothing wrong," she said hoarsely, one hand pressed to the door. "Lord Poole hit me across the head and brought me here. Please, my brother is at the door. He is looking for me. I want to go to him. Please!"

Again, there came nothing but silence to her pleas, leaving Georgiana frightened she was to remain precisely where she was until Lord Poole decided what he was to do with her.

"Are you...are you a lady?"

The voice was uncertain, afraid even, but Georgiana felt a thrill of hope run up her spine as she spoke frantically.

"Yes, I am a lady of quality," she answered, breathless with a rush of anticipation. "I am betrothed to Lord Poole."

"Then why are you locked in there?"

The second voice was more accusing now, the tone less certain and a little wary. Georgiana could not blame them. Were she in their position, she would also feel uncertain.

"I do not know," she answered truthfully. "I was to cry off from my engagement to Lord Poole, and the next thing I know, I am awake here, in this dark room, with no understanding of where I am or why I am here." She shook her head, her throat aching. "Please, my brother, Lord Allerton is at the door now. I have seen him arrive. I know he is looking for me."

She said nothing more, forcing her lips closed as she waited for the two voices to confer about what they ought to do. She wanted to demand that they obey, wanted to force them to do as she asked, but knew she should say nothing of the sort. The fear a servant has over their master's demands could often be a greater impetus than anything else, and she well understood that.

"You say you are a lady of quality, engaged to Lord Poole?" said the first voice, again holding considerable uncertainty. "And he has put you here?"

"My name is Lady Georgiana," she said, a catch in her voice as she tried her best to keep her emotions tightly under control. "My brother is the Earl of Allerton. Please, I do not want to be here. I want to go to my brother."

She heard a whispered conference between the two voices, hearing snatches of their conversation.

"We will lose our positions and have no references!" said the second voice. "What then?"

"I will make sure you both have positions with my

brother's household," Georgiana cried, one hand flat against the door as she fought against desperation, knowing that this was her only opportunity to break free from this room. "With better pay, I assure you. The household is good; my brother is kind. You need not fear for your livelihood."

Closing her eyes, Georgiana began to pray the two women would take pity on her, that they would be willing to do as she asked even in spite of their fears about their master. She held her breath, praying with every ounce of her being that God above would help her break free.

And then, she heard a key scrape in the lock.

Weak and trembling with relief, Georgiana stepped back as the door opened, revealing two young maids standing together wordlessly, their eyes huge as they looked at Georgiana.

"Thank you," she whispered, seeing the candle flickering on a small table to her left. "Thank you." Moving forward slowly, she tried to get her bearings but felt hopelessly lost. "Where am I?"

"In Mr. Forester's house, my lady," squeaked one of the maids, clearly either overwhelmed with what she saw or now terrified of what she had done. "He told us not to come up here to this room, but I'm afraid we were much too curious."

Georgiana leaned heavily on the table but picked up the candle, seeing a dull light coming from one corner of the hallway. "I am very grateful to you both," she answered, weakly. "What are your names?"

"Sophie and Bess, my lady."

Georgiana nodded, giving them both a weak smile. "I will make sure you both have a good position in my brother's house," she promised. "Now, where is the front door to the house?"

The second maid, who had said nothing up until this point, stretched out one hand in the direction of the dull light. "The stairs are that way, my lady," she answered, shakily. "The master told us not to light any candles up this way. You have the only one."

Georgiana nodded and began to make her way towards the light. "Then I must take it," she said hearing the sound of knocking and realizing that her brother and Mr. Lowell had not yet been granted entry to the house. Her heart in her throat, she grasped the handrail and began to make her way down the staircase, afraid that, at any moment, Lord Poole might appear and step in her way.

A figure moved towards the front door, and Georgiana took an instinctive step back, her feet making no noise on the staircase. Her hand still holding the candle, she watched carefully, seeing a man she did not recognize moving slowly towards front door, his steps slow. Keeping as quiet as she could, Georgiana willed the man on, silently begging him to open the door. Her fingers slipped on the silver and gold ribbons that had been tied to the staircase rail, proclaiming the joy of Christmas and the expectation of the happiness that would soon come with the Season—but at this moment, Georgiana felt nothing but abject fear.

"Who is there?"

The man's voice was loud and authoritative, ringing through the house.

"It is Lord Allerton," she heard her brother say, fighting back the urge to rush towards the door and to, somehow, thrust the man out of her way and unlock the door herself. "I must be allowed entry at once."

"I am afraid the master is neither acquainted with nor expecting you," she heard the man say. "Good evening, sir."

The banging on the door resumed with a great deal more force, but as Georgiana watched, the man turned around and slowly made his way back to wherever he had come from. Her heart began to quicken, her nervousness growing steadily. Clearly, this man was not about to let her brother and Mr. Lowell in. None of the staff would do such a thing either, which meant it was solely down to her.

Her hand trembled on the handrail as she began to make her way down the next few stairs. There were only a few candles lit in the hallway below her, but there was enough light to see the key in the door's lock. All she had to do was reach the door and turn the key, for surely then that would allow her brother entry.

"In heaven's name!"

A loud exclamation caught her ears and, as she turned, she saw none other than Lord Poole staring down at her from the top of the staircase. He wore no coat nor cravat, his shirt untucked and his hair in complete disarray. With a shriek, she dropped her candle and raced down the rest of the staircase, hearing him coming thundering behind her.

Another scream ripped from her mouth as she tore towards the front door, her hands going to the key as she tried desperately to turn it. She could hear her brother calling her name, could hear Mr. Lowell's voice loud and frantic as he called for her. At any moment, she expected Lord Poole's hand to grasp at her, turning her head to look as her hands slipped on the key, her fingers damp with nerves.

She had dropped the candle on the staircase and, as such, the flames had caught the Christmas ribbons that had been tied to the handrail. Lord Poole had been forced to stop to put them out, buying her a precious few seconds. He was rushing towards her now, his face bright red with rage, and his eyes narrowed with fury—but just as he put out a hand and grasped her shoulder, the key turned in the lock, and her hands fell from it.

"How dare you?" He had grasped her tightly by the arm now and was physically hauling her away, but before she could react, before she could even say a word, the front door had been thrown open, and both Lord Allerton and Mr. Lowell were standing framed in the doorway.

Georgiana was not quite sure what happened next. She was flung back awkwardly, her head hitting the wall behind her as something crashed and smashed to the ground. Lord Poole's hand was tight on her arm still but, eventually, it began to loosen until she was finally free of him. Her vision was blurry, seeing three figures but not quite being able to make them all out.

Until the voice of her brother reached her ears, and a gentle hand took her own.

"Georgiana?" Lord Allerton's voice was urgent. "Georgiana? Are you quite all right?"

She blinked rapidly, her vision clearing. "Allerton," she breathed, one hand pressed to her head as she squeezed his fingers. "You have found me."

He gave her a tight smile, and she stood up straight, aware of the dull pain in her head but managing to ignore it. "Lord Poole took me here?"

Mr. Lowell, who had been standing over the prone figure of Lord Poole, turned around and looked straight into her eyes, his face a picture of concern. "You are all right, Lady Georgiana?"

Georgiana could not take her eyes from him, wanting to step into his arms, wanting him to hold her tight against him, but knowing she could not do so in front of her brother. "I am well," she answered, wincing just a little as she gestured to her head. "A slight headache, but aside from that..." Looking all about her, she raised her eyes to her brother. "This is not Lord Poole's townhouse?"

"No," her brother grated, angrily. "It is not." He looked to Mr. Lowell, who nodded in silent agreement to whatever it was Lord Allerton was thinking. "Lock the door, Mr. Lowell, and then let us drag Lord Poole into the drawing-room where he might be more obliged to tell us the truth of the matter."

Georgiana was about to ask if they might find something for her to drink when a quiet, quavering voice floated down from the top of the staircase.

"Poole?"

Georgiana froze, looking at Mr. Lowell in shock but remaining utterly silent as they all listened.

"Lord Poole?" came the voice again. "Whatever is the matter? I heard the most awful noise, and I—oh!"

Hardly able to believe what she was seeing, Georgiana stared up at Lady Northcott, who had only just begun to descend the stairs. Her hair was in a simple plait, but aside from that, she was well dressed in a beautiful evening gown. She stared at Georgiana, then moved her gaze to Lord Allerton and finally to Mr. Lowell, her mouth a little ajar and her eyes wide with fright.

"Lady Northcott," Mr. Lowell breathed, glancing towards Lord Poole, who was still semi-conscious from the blow to the head that Lord Allerton had planted on him. "I see."

Georgiana shook her head in disbelief, thinking to herself that things were becoming all the more convoluted.

"Might you join us in the drawing-room, Lady Northcott?" Lord Allerton said in a tone that was not at all open to questioning. "At once."

Lady Northcott swallowed hard, her mouth opening and closing in an evident attempt to express herself, but in the end, she said nothing at all. Quite afraid, she stepped down the staircase, holding the handrail tightly as she did so. Her chin lifted as she drew near Lord Allerton, although she did not once look towards Georgiana.

"The drawing-room, if you please," Lord Allerton said gesturing for the lady to step forward. Lady Northcott held his gaze for a moment longer, then, seeming to quail beneath it, did as she was instructed and moved forward without hesitation—although she did not so much as glance at Lord Poole, nor at Mr. Lowell.

A sudden realization dawned. "This is her townhouse," Georgiana breathed, looking at her brother, who was nodding grimly. "That is what you think?"

"I believe so," Lord Allerton answered, patting Georgiana gently on the shoulder, although his expression remained the same. "I think there is more to this situation than there first appears, Georgiana." He turned to her a little more, looking at her directly in the eye. "Do you wish to return home? I can leave Mr. Lowell here and take you to Lady Allerton directly."

She shook her head, now wanting to find out the truth behind Lord Poole's attempts to steal her from her brother as well as his association with Lady Northcott. "I would like to remain here," she told him with a small smile that seemed to bolster her courage. "I want to know the truth."

He nodded. "Very well," he said, turning to Mr. Lowell. "Mr. Lowell, if you might take my sister into the drawing-room and sit with her there." He eyed Lord Poole, who was now groaning and attempting to sit up. "I will ensure Lord Poole makes his way into the room without delay."

Mr. Lowell smiled gently at Georgiana, clearly trying to reassure her. "But of course," he said softly in answer to Lord Allerton's question. Leaving Lord Poole to be dealt with by her brother, Mr. Lowell came towards Georgiana, his hand outstretched. Georgiana took it at once, feeling the surge of warmth rush all through her as their fingers met.

"You have done very well, Lady Georgiana," he murmured, his other hand settling about her waist as he drew her into him, allowing her to lean on him, a breath of relief escaping from her. "I can't tell you just how relieved I am to know you are safe."

Looking up into his face, Georgiana felt her heart swell with affection and love, knowing she had no choice in the matter as to how she now felt.

"You cannot know just how glad I was to see your face," she answered as he led her slowly towards the drawing-room. "I feared I would never see it again."

He smiled at her, his eyes holding hers. "If I had my way, you should never be lost to me again," he said softly as they left Lord Poole and Lord Allerton behind. He said nothing more, those words burning in her mind as she held his gaze, seeing nothing but him. Her relief at being freed from Lord Poole overwhelmed her. Her future was no longer dark, no longer wreathed in the shadows of loneliness and pain. There would be no Lord Poole; there would be no terror he would strike out at her, would leave her to bear her pain alone. There was nothing now other than a fresh hope, a new light. A light that would find its fulfillment in Mr. Lowell's arms.

CHAPTER TWELVE

"So, Lord Poole..."

Oliver watched as Lord Allerton spoke gravely to his acquaintance. He himself felt fit to burst with anger, although he was managing to keep such feelings well under control. With Lady Georgiana beside him, his relief was so great it overwhelmed the desire to plant a facer on Lord Poole, knowing full well that had he the opportunity, he would have done precisely the same as Lord Allerton and would have knocked Lord Poole to the ground.

His heart turned over in his chest as he recalled how he had been pounding on the door along with Lord Allerton, only to hear the scream of what they presumed to be Lady Georgiana. Both of them had become almost frantic in their desire to have the door opened, with Oliver thinking of smashing in one of the windows and crawling through, should it come to it.

Thankfully, the key had turned, and within moments, both he and Lord Allerton had managed to make their way through. Seeing Lady Georgiana in Lord Poole's grasp had set fire to Oliver's anger, and he had grabbed out at the man, pulling him away from Lady Georgiana, although Lord Poole had not let go. They had knocked into a small table, with a vase of flowers smashing to the floor and, in an attempt to force Lord Poole away from Lady Georgiana, Lord Allerton had punched the fellow hard in the face, knocking him to the ground.

How glad he was now that Lady Georgiana was safe.

"What do you want, Allerton?"

Lord Poole's eyes were angry, his face red on one side where Lord Allerton had punched him.

"I want to know why you took my sister away," Lord Allerton said with more calmness than Oliver had expected. "Why you decided to kidnap her and take her to your mistress's house."

Lady Georgiana gasped, her eyes flaring wide as a slight shock ran through Oliver. Lady Northcott was Lord Poole's mistress?

Lord Poole threw his head back and laughed gruffly as though Lord Allerton had made the most ridiculous assertion.

"Lady Northcott is *not* my mistress," he said darkly as Lady Northcott's eyes began to spill with tears. "And as for your sister, Lord Allerton, I think you will find that the fault is with her."

Oliver squeezed Lady Georgiana's hand tightly, seeing how she jerked forward, clearly wanting to refute this, but he knew there was no need. Lord Allerton was not about to believe his acquaintance over his sister, and besides which, there was no reason for anyone to do what Lord Poole had done. Lady Georgiana looked at him, her face a little flushed, but Oliver merely smiled at her, wanting to reassure her as best he could. There was no need for her to defend herself.

"What fault is that?" Lord Allerton asked softly, his voice seeming to fill the room even though he was speaking quietly. "What was it my sister did that merited such dire consequences?"

Lord Poole sniffed and looked away. "She was to cry off."

"As is her right," Lord Allerton said his voice now dangerously low. "She was permitted to make such a decision, Lord Poole. Why, then, would you try to stop her?"

Lord Poole lifted his chin, clearly not in the least bit sorrowful over his actions. "I made an agreement with you," he stated, unequivocally. "I am not a gentleman used to having such agreements abolished."

"Regardless," Lord Allerton interrupted before Lord Poole could say more. "If Lady Georgiana wished to step away from the agreement, then she is permitted to do so. I would not have prevented her."

Oliver glanced at Lady Georgiana, hearing her swift intake of breath. Had she not known that her brother would have permitted her to do such a thing? Or had she feared it was quite impossible?

"But that is where you and I are quite different, Lord Allerton," Lord Poole said icily. "You are weak and soft-hearted. I am not."

"And so you would kidnap Lady Georgiana to get

what you want?" Oliver interrupted, unable to prevent himself from speaking. "You would do this dire thing to gain what you wanted?"

Lord Poole shot him a hard glance and then looked away, an arrogant smirk on his face. "I would not expect you to understand, *Mr.* Lowell," he said emphasizing Oliver's title. "The shame and the embarrassment that would be brought would sting my family name and might have society mocking me for a time."

Oliver closed his eyes, biting back a sharp retort. For a gentleman to go so far as to steal a young lady away in order to avoid a few months of whispers was something he simply could not understand.

"And Lady Northcott?" Lord Allerton asked, looking towards the lady. "What is it you have to do with this?"

Lady Northcott's eyes widened, her expression one of sweet innocence. "I cannot understand what you are speaking of, Lord Allerton!" she exclaimed in evident confusion. "I did not even know Lady Georgiana was here until I saw her standing in the hallway with you."

Oliver squeezed Lady Georgiana's hand. "Is that true?" he asked in a low voice. "Did you hear her or see her beforehand?"

Lady Georgiana shook her head, looking a little upset. "I was hit on the head, I think," she said softly, her words sending another slice of anger through Oliver, which he forcibly contained by gritting his teeth. "I only awoke a short time before I saw you from the window."

Oliver, remembering how he and Lord Allerton had seen a faint shadow moving in a window whilst hearing a loud knocking sound, finally understood what that had been. "I see," he answered, taking in long breaths to quell his anger a little more. "You have been very poorly treated, Lady Georgiana."

"I do not believe you were unaware of my sister's presence in this house, Lady Northcott," Lord Allerton said firmly as Lady Northcott continued to bat her eyes at him. "She was held here in one of your rooms and—"

"This is not my house, Lord Allerton," Lady Northcott interrupted with a small smile that baited Oliver's anger all the more. "Surely you know that?"

Lord Allerton merely raised an eyebrow and looked at Lord Poole, who turned his head away. "It is your brother's townhouse, then, Lord Poole," he said as Oliver watched with satisfaction as the smile on Lady Northcott's face fell to the floor. "Which does not explain why you were above stairs, Lady Northcott."

"And Lord Poole came from upstairs," Lady Georgiana interrupted, her voice rising. "As you did shortly afterward, Lady Northcott."

"We were just visiting," Lady Northcott protested, her cheeks now a delicate pink. "Surely we are all aware of my enjoyment of a gentleman's company?" She shrugged whilst Lady Georgiana blushed furiously. "It is not something I—"

"And your brother, Lord Poole?" Lord Allerton interrupted. "Where is he this evening?"

Lord Poole cleared his throat, a supercilious look on his face. Clearly, he did not see any merit in lying to Lord Allerton, merely shrugging at the question. "He is out of town at present."

"Wait." Oliver rose to his feet, an awareness hitting

him as he caught the attention of everyone in the room. "The necklace." He turned to Lady Georgiana, who was watching him intently, her eyes wide with astonishment. "That night, Lady Georgiana, when you helped rescue me from that delicate situation."

Lady Georgiana blinked, then began to nod as she recalled things. "The necklace was placed in your pocket by a footman, I think."

"That is what I believed, yes," he said as Lady Northcott began to frown. "Lady Northcott feigned a deep upset it was lost, only for it to be found in the corner of the room...thanks to you, Lady Georgiana." He gave her a quick smile, his mind working furiously. "You placed it there deliberately, Lady Northcott. You wanted me to be seen as a thief and a charlatan. At the time, both myself and Lady Georgiana believed it was because I had refused your advances, because I did not wish to become one of your many gentleman callers, but what if it was for another reason altogether?"

A gasp came from Lady Georgiana, evidencing she too had come to understand what he meant.

"You are being quite ridiculous, Mr. Lowell," Lady Northcott exclaimed with a wave of her hand that was an attempt at dismissing him. "I would never behave in such a devious fashion!"

"Your agreement with Lord Poole to kidnap Lady Georgiana when your first ploy did not work out as expected would say otherwise," he told her, seeing how pale she went. "Lord Poole, I expect, came to seek your help—for a tidy sum, I might imagine. I presume he saw Lady Georgiana and I speaking, and mayhap feared there was an intimacy there he would have to fight against. Perhaps he did not want anyone speaking of it, did not want Lady Georgiana to even *continue* with such an association for fear of what it might do to his reputation."

"And so, he asked you to ruin Mr. Lowell's good name," Lady Georgiana breathed, staring at Lady North-cott. "And you found a good way to do so. You attempted to make it appear as though he had stolen the necklace."

"Which was usurped by Lady Georgiana," Oliver continued, glaring hard at Lord Poole, who had gone a rather sickly shade of gray. "And when that did not work, and even though you had an arrangement with Lord Allerton, you still were afraid you might not have what you wanted. So you threatened Lady Georgiana. You told her to stay far away from me, otherwise all manner of shame and scandal would fall on not only my head but that of my cousin."

Lord Allerton rose to his feet, his face now wreathed with anger. "And when Lady Georgiana was convinced not to be afraid of such threats, you decided to take matters into your own hands," he finished, as Lord Poole seemed to sink a little further into the chair, no longer wearing his haughty smile. "That is utterly despicable, Lord Poole!"

Lord Poole lifted his chin, but the mask of arrogance was slipping. "I am betrothed to Lady Georgiana!"

"You are not betrothed any longer!" Lord Allerton shouted, his rage more than apparent now. "How dare you treat my sister in such a way? What cruelty you have shown to her, as well as to Mr. Lowell? You are not deserving of Lady Georgiana, Lord Poole, and I shall make certain that all of society knows it!"

Lord Poole went sheet white in an instant. His hands began to scramble on the chair arms as he tried to get to his feet, but Lord Allerton was already there, glaring down at him.

"You have nothing further to say, Lord Poole," he grated as Oliver reached out one hand towards Lady Georgiana, seeing how she had begun to tremble. "The society you hold so dear will turn on you. Everyone will know what you have tried to do."

Lord Poole began to stammer, holding out one hand beseechingly. "But there will be whispers about your sister!" he exclaimed as though this would make any difference. "Surely you cannot—"

"I would accept such gossip if it were to ensure that all of society knows the darkness of your character," Lady Georgiana said, her hand tightening hard on Oliver's as she spoke with strength and dignity. "I am glad to be free of you, Lord Poole, and I will accept whatever consequences come from telling the *beau monde* what has occurred." She said nothing more but began to walk quickly towards the door, with Oliver walking beside her, her hand in his. The quiet strength of her amazed him, the beauty of her determined spirits capturing his heart all over again. She was magnificent, and he found himself entirely lost.

The return journey back to Lord Allerton's townhouse was a quiet one. Lady Georgiana said very little, but her hand held fast to his under the blankets that Lord Allerton insisted on piling onto her. She smiled at her brother but rested her head back against the squabs, clearly exhausted. Oliver felt his throat constrict with the realization he would have to leave her behind. His boat to America would sail shortly after Christmas, meaning he would never see her again.

Not unless he bared his heart and offered her his hand. It would mean leaving behind all she knew, all those she loved, and Oliver knew all too well it might not be a decision she could easily make. Now was not the time to ask her such a question, however, given just how tired she was. There would need to be a few days to recover before he could even begin to consider speaking to her about such delicate matters.

"I will return to my cousin's house," he said softly as the hackney came to a stop. "You will need to rest, Lady Georgiana. I am very glad to see you back here safely."

Her eyes glistened as she looked at him, and for a moment, Oliver thought Lady Georgiana might ask him to come in, might ask him to stay. But then she let out a long breath, sighed, and nodded.

"Thank you for all of your help, Mr. Lowell," Lord Allerton said gravely. "I cannot tell you how much I appreciate all you did."

Oliver cleared his throat, feeling the weight of what he had left unspoken resting on his shoulders. "Not at all," he said reluctantly letting go of Lady Georgiana's hand. "I hope I will see you again very soon, Lady Georgiana."

Her hand caught his again, holding it tightly. "Come to call on Christmas Eve," she said softly, looking into his eyes. "Bring your cousin and her husband if you wish, but do say you will come. My brother is having a small soiree that will lead us from Christmas Eve into Christmas Day, and I am sure you would be welcome."

"*More* than welcome," Lord Allerton said, nodding. "I would be glad to see you there, Mr. Lowell."

Smiling and feeling his heart lifting with a surge of happiness, Oliver accepted the invitation. "I would be glad to," he answered, seeing how Lady Georgiana let out a long breath of evident relief. "Until then, Lady Georgiana. Lord Allerton."

"Until then," Lady Georgiana answered as the hackney driver pulled open the door. "And thank you again, Mr. Lowell, for all you did this evening. You do not know just how grateful I am for your help."

He said nothing but watched her climb from the hackney, feeling his heart go with her as she climbed the steps and into the house. He loved her desperately, he knew, and even a short separation pained him terribly. How, then, was he meant to leave for America when the lady he loved remained here? His heart and his head filled with questions, Oliver closed the door and rested his head back, his eyes closing. Christmas Eve could not come soon enough.

EPILOGUE

"Mr. Lowell."

Georgiana practically breathed his name, her cheeks flushing as he came into the room and grasped her outstretched hands. His eyes searched her face for a moment before, finally, he broke into a smile.

"You look quite wonderful, Lady Georgiana," he told her, clearly relieved she did not appear to be ill or weak from her trial. "You are well recovered, I hope?"

"More than recovered," she answered honestly, expressing the relief that had come from knowing she was now free from Lord Poole's clutches. "I am so very glad you could be here on Christmas Eve." Her eyes fastened on his face, seeing how his gaze went around the room. All the greenery for the festive season had been brought in earlier that day, as tradition would have it, and she and Lady Allerton had spent some time making wreaths and folding ribbons to bring extra festive cheer after what had been a very difficult few weeks.

"Another mistletoe bough I see," Mr. Lowell murmured, making Georgiana's heart race with a sudden excitement. "And good gracious, what a roaring fire!" Instinctively, he moved towards it, and Georgiana went with him, glad that her brother and sister-in-law had thought only to invite a small number of guests. It was more intimate this way, more welcoming and friendly. And, given the way the news of Lord Poole's actions had spread through society, Georgiana was all the more relieved.

"It is the Yule Log," Georgiana said, briefly explaining the tradition. "The staff did very well in finding such an excellent log this year. I am sure it will burn for the twelve nights it is expected to." She smiled up at him, seeing his eyes grow sorrowful and felt her stomach twist with anxiety. "Is something wrong?"

Mr. Lowell let out a long, slow breath and, with a quick glance over his shoulder, moved a little closer to her and settled his hand over their joined ones. "Twelve nights. That is as many days as I have left here."

She caught her breath, staring up at him as a sudden rush of sorrow ran over her. "You have booked your passage?"

"I have," he said a little heavily. "I cannot stay any longer. I must go back to Boston to look after my business affairs."

Georgiana nodded slowly. She had known this was coming, yet still, it crushed her spirits.

"I am sorry to have to leave you," Mr. Lowell continued, a trifle quieter now. "It makes me wretched to think of leaving you behind."

She looked up at him sharply, wondering if he was about to say something more, but he only glanced away, appearing a little uncertain.

You began to find your courage when Lord Poole took you away, Georgiana told herself sternly. *Do not give it up now. Seize hold of it and speak to Mr. Lowell of your heart!*

Taking in a deep breath, Georgiana turned and pulled Mr. Lowell towards the door. She was courting scandal in being so obvious, quite certain that almost every eye was on her as she disappeared through the door with Mr. Lowell behind her but finding she did not care a jot. Without saying a word, she led Mr. Lowell into the library and shut the door tightly behind them both.

"Lady Georgiana," Mr. Lowell exclaimed, something in his expression that told her he already knew what she was going to say. "Is it not *very* improper for a young lady to be alone with a gentleman?"

She tipped her head, planting her hands on her hips. "It is," she answered. "But this is a very important matter, and I will take the risk." The corner of her mouth lifted in a small smile. "Besides which, given almost everyone in London knows what Lord Poole did, I am already well whispered about." Lifting one shoulder in a small shrug, she held her head high. "Not that I give any thought to it," she finished with a touch of defiance. "It is worth it to save any other poor creature from his hands."

"You are strong of both heart and mind," Mr. Lowell answered warmly, his eyes holding to hers. "I admire it."

"I have not always been so," she replied, feeling her heart hammering against her chest. "In fact, I am not feeling particularly strong of mind at the present, even though my heart is urging me forward."

Something changed at that moment. Something shifted between them, the air seeming to grow thick as she stopped only a tiny distance away from Mr. Lowell. She could feel his breath brushing across her skin as she lifted her head, looking deeply into his eyes and praying he could see the love in her heart.

"You say you are already touched by scandal, Georgiana," Mr. Lowell began, reaching out one hand and taking hers tightly in his own. "I don't want there to be yet more whispers about you throughout all of society, but there is something I must ask." His voice was low, the words he spoke sending glorious tremors over her skin.

"Yes, Mr. Lowell?" she asked, looking up into his face and feeling her heart lifting towards the skies, chasing away any last embers of fear and doubt. "What is it you must ask?"

Closing his eyes, he leaned forward until his forehead rested gently on hers. There was such beauty in this moment, such wonderful contentment that Georgiana wanted to wrap it up tightly and hold it within herself. She did not want it to end, feeling her heart reach out towards his, tying themselves together as one.

"I have spoken unclearly in the past, but I will tell you the unequivocal truth now," Mr. Lowell murmured, his free hand now settling on her waist. "I must return to America, Georgiana, but I don't want to go without you." His eyes opened, and Georgiana caught her breath. "If you marry me quickly, then we can leave for America together. I know that all of society will be shocked by your actions, I know that rumors and gossip will pour out on your family, but I cannot bear to leave you behind." Taking a breath, he pulled her a little closer. "It will be a new life for you, Georgiana. There will be things that are unfamiliar, things that are difficult, but my love for you will carry you through it until my home becomes your home too." Lifting his hand, he brushed it down her cheek, and Georgiana closed her eyes, her happiness burning through every part of her. "I love you, Georgiana," he finished, almost tripping over his words in his haste to speak them to her. "I love you desperately."

"As I love you."

Those four short words were all Mr. Lowell needed. With an infinite gentleness and yet with a heat of passion, he pressed his lips to hers and kissed her. Georgiana leaned into him, her arms about his neck and her heart fully his. She had already made her decision the day she had spoken to Lady Allerton about all she felt. She had known she would set her back to England and go to America with Mr. Lowell, should he ask her. Her brother had already assented, with Lady Allerton thrilled to know that Georgiana would be so happily contented in her marriage. All she had needed to wait for was for Mr. Lowell to ask.

"It will be a very different Christmas next year," he told her, lifting his lips from hers for just a moment. "But you shall always have me beside you."

"And that is all I shall need," she promised, laughing softly as she heard the bells began to chime, bringing Christmas Eve into Christmas Day.

. . .

I hope you enjoyed Georgiana and Mr Lowell's story. I have another Christmas story on preorder...Check out A Family for Christmas

MY DEAR READER

Thank you for reading and supporting my books! I hope this story brought you some escape from the real world into the always captivating Regency world. A good story, especially one with a happy ending, just brightens your day and makes you feel good! If you enjoyed the book, would you leave a review on Amazon? Reviews are always appreciated.

Below is a complete list of all my books! Why not click and see if one of them can keep you entertained for a few hours?

The Duke's Daughters Series
The Duke's Daughters: A Sweet Regency Romance Boxset
A Rogue for a Lady
My Restless Earl
Rescued by an Earl
In the Arms of an Earl
The Reluctant Marquess (Prequel)

A Smithfield Market Regency Romance
The Smithfield Market Romances: A Sweet Regency
Romance Boxset
The Rogue's Flower
Saved by the Scoundrel
Mending the Duke
The Baron's Malady

The Returned Lords of Grosvenor Square
The Returned Lords of Grosvenor Square: A Regency
Romance Boxset
The Waiting Bride
The Long Return
The Duke's Saving Grace
A New Home for the Duke

The Spinsters Guild
A New Beginning
The Disgraced Bride
A Gentleman's Revenge
A Foolish Wager

Mistletoe Magic: A Regency Romance
Home for Christmas Series Page
A Family for Christmas
Love and Christmas Wishes: Three Regency Romance
Novellas

Collections with other Regency Authors
Love, One Regency Spring
Love a Lord in Summer

Please continue on to the next page for a preview of the first book in The Spinsters Guild series, **A New Beginning**! If you have already read A New Beginning, please try The Returned Lords of Grosvenor Square: A Regency Romance Boxset. It will keep you entertained for hours!

Happy Reading!

All my love,

A SNEAK PEEK OF A NEW BEGINNING

CHAPTER ONE

"Good evening, Miss Taylor."

Miss Emily Taylor, daughter to the Viscount Chesterton, kept her gaze low to the ground, her stomach knotting. The gentleman who had greeted her was, at this present moment, looking at her with something akin to a leer, his balding head already gleaming in the candlelight.

"Good evening, Lord Smithton," she murmured, hearing the grunt from her father than indicated she should be doing more than simply acknowledging the gentleman's presence. The last thing Emily wished to do, however, was to encourage the man any further. He was, to her eyes, grotesque, and certainly not a suitable match for someone who had only recently made her debut, even *if* he was a Marquess.

"Emily is delighted to see you this evening," her father said, giving Emily a small push forward. "I am certain she will be glad to dance with you whenever you wish!"

Emily closed her eyes, resisting the urge to step back from the fellow, in the knowledge that should she do so, her father would make certain that consequences would follow. She could not bring herself to speak, almost feeling Lord Smithton's eyes roving over her form as she opened her eyes and kept her gaze low.

"You know very well that I would be more than pleased to accompany you to the floor," Lord Smithton said, his voice low and filled with apparent longing. Emily suppressed a shudder, forcing herself to put her hand out and let her dance card drop from her wrist. Lord Smithton, however, did not grasp her dance card but took her hand in his, making a gasp escape from her mouth. The swift intake of breath from behind her informed Emily that she was not alone in her surprise and shock, for her mother also was clearly very upset that Lord Smithton had behaved in such an improper fashion. Her father, however, said nothing and, in the silence that followed, allowed himself a small chuckle.

Emily wanted to weep. It was obvious that her father was not about to say a single word about Lord Smithton's improper behavior. Instead, it seemed he was encouraging it. Her heart ached with the sorrow that came from having a father who cared so little for her that he would allow impropriety in front of so many of the *beau monde*. Her reputation could be stained from such a thing, whispers spread about her, and yet her father would stand by and allow them to go about her without even a twinge of concern.

Most likely, this was because his intention was for Emily to wed Lord Smithton. It had been something

Emily had begun to suspect during these last two weeks, for Lord Smithton had been present at the same social gatherings as she had attended with her parents, and her father had always insisted that she greet him. Nothing had been said as yet, however, which came as something of a relief, but deep down, Emily feared that her father would simply announce one day that she was engaged to the old, leering Lord Smithton.

"Wonderful," Lord Smithton murmured, finally letting go of Emily's hand and grasping her dance card. "I see that you have no others as yet, Miss Taylor."

"We have only just arrived," said Emily's mother, from just behind Emily. "That is why –"

"I am certain that Lord Smithton does not need to know such things," Lord Chesterton interrupted, silencing Emily's mother immediately. "He is clearly grateful that Emily has not yet had her head turned by any other gentleman as yet."

Closing her eyes tightly, Emily forced herself to breathe normally, aware of how Lord Smithton chuckled at this. She did not have any feelings of attraction or even fondness for Lord Smithton but yet her father was stating outright that she was interested in Lord Smithton's attentions!

"I have chosen the quadrille, the waltz and the supper dance, Miss Taylor."

Emily's eyes shot open, and she practically jerked back the dance card from Lord Smithton's hands, preventing him from finishing writing his name in the final space. Her father stiffened beside her, her mother gasping in shock, but Emily did not allow either reaction to prevent her from keeping her dance card away from Lord Smithton.

"I am afraid I cannot permit such a thing, Lord Smithton," she told him plainly, her voice shaking as she struggled to find the confidence to speak with the strength she needed. "Three dances would, as you know, send many a tongue wagging and I cannot allow such a thing to happen. I am quite certain you will understand." She lifted her chin, her stomach twisting this way and that in fright as Lord Smithton narrowed his eyes and glared at her.

"My daughter is quite correct, Lord Smithton," Lady Chesterton added, settling a cold hand on Emily's shoulder. "Three dances are, as you know, something that the *ton* will notice and discuss without dissention."

Emily held her breath, seeing how her father and Lord Smithton exchanged a glance. Her eyes began to burn with unshed tears but she did not allow a single one to fall. She was trying to be strong, was she not? Therefore, she could not allow herself to show Lord Smithton even a single sign of weakness.

"I suppose that is to be understood," Lord Smithton said, eventually, forcing a breath of relief to escape from Emily's chest, weakening her. "Given that I have not made my intentions towards you clear, Miss Taylor."

The weakness within her grew all the more. "Intentions?" she repeated, seeing the slow smile spreading across Lord Smithton's face and feeling almost sick with the horror of what was to come.

Lord Smithton took a step closer to her and reached for her hand, which Emily was powerless to refuse. His eyes were fixed on hers, his tongue running across his lower lip for a moment before he spoke.

"Your father and I have been in discussions as regards your dowry and the like, Miss Taylor," he explained, his hand tightening on hers. "We should come to an agreement very soon, I am certain of it."

Emily closed her eyes tightly, feeling her mother's hand still resting on her shoulder and forcing herself to focus on it, to feel the support that she needed to manage this moment and all the emotions that came with it.

"We shall be wed before Season's end," Lord Smithton finished, grandly, as though Emily would be delighted with such news. "We shall be happy and content, shall we not, Miss Taylor?"

The lump in Emily's throat prevented her from saying anything. She wanted to tell Lord Smithton that he had not even asked her to wed him, had not considered her answer, but the words would not come to her lips. Of course, she would have no choice in the matter. Her father would make certain of that.

"You are speechless, of course," Lord Smithton chuckled, as her father grunted his approval. "I know that this will come as something of a surprise that I have denied myself towards marrying someone such as you, but I have no doubt that we shall get along rather famously." His chuckle became dark, his hand tightening on hers until it became almost painful. "You are an obedient sort, are you not?"

"She is," Emily heard her father say, as she opened her eyes to see Lord Smithton's gaze running over her form. She had little doubt as to what he was referring to, for her mother had already spoken to her about what a husband would require from his wife, and the very thought terrified her.

"Take her, now."

Lord Smithton let go of Emily's hand and gestured towards Lady Chesterton, as though she were his to order about.

"Take her to seek some refreshment. She looks somewhat pale." He laughed and then turned away to speak to Emily's father again, leaving Emily and her mother standing together.

Emily's breathing was becoming ragged, her heart trembling within her as she struggled to fight against the dark clouds that were filling her heart and mind. To be married to such an odious gentleman as Lord Smithton was utterly terrifying. She would have no joy in her life any longer, not even an ounce of happiness in her daily living. Was this her doing? Was it because she had not been strong enough to stand up to her own father and refuse to do as he asked? Her hands clenched hard, her eyes closing tightly as she fought to contain the sheer agony that was deep within her heart.

"My dear girl, I am so dreadfully sorry."

Lady Chesterton touched her arm but Emily jerked away, her eyes opening. "I cannot marry Lord Smithton, Mama."

"You have no choice," Lady Chesterton replied, sadly, her own eyes glistening. "I have tried to speak to your father but you know the sort of gentleman he is."

"Then I shall run away," Emily stated, fighting against the desperation that filled her. "I cannot remain."

Lady Chesterton said nothing for a moment or two, allowing Emily to realize the stupidity of what she had said. There was no-one else to whom she could turn to, no-one else to whom she might escape. The only choices that were open to her were either to do as her father asked or to find another who might marry her instead – and the latter gave her very little hope.

Unless Lord Havisham....

The thought was pushed out of her mind before she could begin to consider it. She had become acquainted with Lord Havisham over the few weeks she had been in London and he had appeared very attentive. He always sought her out to seek a dance or two, found her conversation engaging and had even called upon her on more than one occasion. But to ask him to consider marrying her was something that Emily simply could not contemplate. He would think her rude, foolish and entirely improper, particularly when she could not be certain that he had any true affection for her.

But if you do nothing, then Lord Smithton will have his way.

"Emily."

Her mother's voice pulled her back to where she stood, seeing the pity and the helplessness in her mother's eyes and finding herself filling with despair as she considered her future.

"I do not want to marry Lord Smithton," Emily said again, tremulously. "He is improper, rude and I find myself afraid of him." She saw her mother drop her head, clearly struggling to find any words to encourage Emily. "What am I to do, mama?"

"I – I do not know." Lady Chesterton looked up slowly, a single tear running down her cheek. "I would save you from this if I could, Emily but there is nothing I can do or say that will prevent your father from forcing this upon you."

Emily felt as though a vast, dark chasm had opened up underneath her feet, pulling her down into it until she could barely breathe. The shadows seemed to fill her lungs, reaching in to tug at her heart until it beat so quickly that she felt as though she might faint.

"I must go," Emily whispered, reaching out to grasp her mother's hand for a moment. "I need a few minutes alone." She did not wait for her mother to say anything, to give her consent or refusal, but hurried away without so much as a backward look. She walked blindly through the crowd of guests, not looking to the left or to the right but rather straight ahead, fixing her gaze on her goal. The open doors that led to the dark gardens.

The cool night air brushed at her hot cheeks but Emily barely noticed. Wrapping her arms about her waist, she hurried down the steps and then sped across the grass, not staying on the paths that wound through the gardens themselves. She did not know where she was going, only that she needed to find a small, dark, quiet space where she might allow herself to think and to cry without being seen.

She soon found it. A small arbor kept her enclosed as she sank down onto the small wooden bench. No sound other than that of strains of music and laughter from the ballroom reached her ears. Leaning forward, Emily felt herself begin to crumble from within, her heart aching and her mind filled with despair. There was no way out. There was nothing she could do. She would have to marry Lord Smithton and, in doing so, would bring herself more sadness and pain than she had ever felt before.

There was no-one to rescue her. There was no-one to save her. She was completely and utterly alone.

CHAPTER TWO

*T*hree days later and Emily had stopped her weeping and was now staring at herself in the mirror, taking in the paleness of her cheeks and the dullness of her eyes.

Her father had only just now informed her that she was to be wed by the Season's end and was now to consider herself engaged. There had been no discussion. There had been not even a thought as to what she herself might feel as regarded Lord Smithton. It had simply been a matter of course. She was to do as her father had directed, as she had been taught to do.

Emily swallowed hard, closing her eyes tightly as another wave of tears crashed against her closed lids. Was this to be her end? Married to Lord Smithton, a gentleman whom she despised, and allowing herself to be treated in any way he chose? It would be a continuation of her life as it was now. No consideration, no thought was given to her. Expected to do as she was instructed without question – and no doubt the consequences would be severe for her if she did not do as Lord Smithton expected.

A shudder ran through her and Emily opened her eyes. For the first time, a small flickering flame of anger ignited and began to burn within her. Was she simply going to allow this to be her life? Was she merely going to step aside and allow Lord Smithton and her father to come to this arrangement without her acceptance? Was she truly as weak as all that?

Heat climbed up her spine and into her face. Weak was a word to describe her, yes. She *was* weak. She had tried, upon occasion, to do as she pleased instead of what her father had demanded of her and the punishment each time had broken her spirit all the more until she had not even a single thought about disobeying him. It had been what had led to this circumstance. If she had been stronger, if she had been more willing to accept the consequences of refusing to obey her father without question without allowing such a thing to break her spirit, then would she be as she was now?

"Then mayhap there is a time yet to change my circumstances."

The voice that came from her was weak and tremulous but with a lift of her chin, Emily told herself that she needed to try and find some courage if she was to find any hope of escaping Lord Smithton. And the only thought she had was that of Lord Havisham.

Viscount Havisham was, of course, lower in title and wealth than the Marquess of Smithton, but that did not matter to Emily. They had discovered a growing acquaintance between them, even though it was not often that her father had let her alone to dance and converse with another gentleman. It had been a blessing that the requests to call upon her had come at a time when her father had been resting from the events of the previous evening, for her and her mother had been able to arrange for him to call when Lord Chesterton had been gone from the house. However, nothing of consequence had ever been shared between them and he certainly had not, as yet, made his request to court her but mayhap it had simply been too soon for such a decision. Regardless, Emily could not pretend that they did not enjoy a comfortable acquaintance, with easy conversation and many warm glances shared between them. In truth, her heart fluttered whenever she laid eyes upon him, for his handsome features and his broad smile had a profound effect upon her.

It was her only chance to escape from Lord Smithton. She had to speak to Lord Havisham and lay her heart bare. She had to trust that he too had a fondness for her, in the same way that she had found her affections touched by him. Else what else was she to do?

Lifting her chin, Emily closed her eyes and took in a long breath to steady herself. After a moment of quiet reflection, she rose and made her way to the writing table in the corner of the bedchamber, sitting down carefully and picking up her quill.

∽

"Miss Taylor."

Emily's breath caught as she looked up into Lord

Havisham's face. His dark blue eyes held a hint of concern, his smile somewhat tensed as he bowed in greeting.

"Lord Havisham," she breathed, finding even his very presence to be overwhelming. "You received my note, then."

"I did," he replied, with a quick smile, although a frown began to furrow his brow. "You said that it was of the utmost importance that we spoke this evening."

Emily nodded, looking about her and seeing that her father was making his way up the small staircase towards the card room, walking alongside Lord Smithton. Their engagement was to be announced later this evening and Emily knew she had to speak to Lord Havisham before that occurred.

"I know this is most untoward, but might we speak in private?" she asked, reaching out and surreptitiously putting her hand on his arm, battling against the fear of impropriety. She had done this much, she told herself. Therefore, all she had to do was continue on as she had begun and her courage might be rewarded.

Lord Havisham hesitated. "That may be a little...."

Emily blushed furiously, knowing that to speak alone with a gentleman was not at all correct, for it could bring damaging consequences to them both – but for her, at this moment, she did not find it to be a particularly concerning issue, given that she was to be married to Lord Smithton if he did not do anything.

"It is of the greatest importance, as I have said," she replied, quickly, praying that he would consent. "Please, Lord Havisham, it will not take up more than a few minutes of your time." Seeing him hesitate even more, she bit her lip. "Surely you must know me well enough to know that I would not force you into anything, Lord Havisham," she pleaded, noting how his eyes darted away from hers, a slight flush now in his cheeks. "There is enough of a friendship between us, is there not?"

Lord Havisham nodded and then sighed "I am sorry, Miss Taylor," he replied, quietly, looking at her. "You are quite right. Come. The gardens will be quiet."

Walking away from her mother – who did not do anything to hinder Emily's departure, Emily felt such an overwhelming sense of relief that it was all she could do to keep her composure. Surely Lord Havisham, with his goodness and kind nature, would see the struggle that faced her and seek to do what he could to bring her aid? Surely he had something of an affection in his heart for her? But would it be enough?

"Now," Lord Havisham began, as they stepped outside. "What is it that troubles you so, Miss Taylor?"

Now that it came to it, Emily found her mouth going dry and her heart pounding so furiously that she could barely speak. She looked up at Lord Havisham, seeing his features only slightly in the darkness of the evening and found herself desperately trying to say even a single word.

"It is....." Closing her eyes, she halted and dragged in air, knowing that she was making a complete cake of herself.

"I am to be wed to Lord Smithton," she managed to say, her words tumbling over each other in an attempt to be spoken. "I have no wish to marry him but my father insists upon it." Opening her eyes, she glanced warily up at Lord Havisham and saw his expression freeze.

Find out what happens next between Emily and Lord Havisham in the book, available in the Kindle Store A New Beginning

JOIN MY MAILING LIST

Sign up for my newsletter to stay up to date on new releases, contests, giveaways, freebies, and deals!

Free book with signup!

Monthly Facebook Giveaways! Books and Amazon gift cards!
Join me on Facebook: https://www. facebook.com/rosepearsonauthor

Website: www.RosePearsonAuthor.com

Follow me on Goodreads: Author Page

You can also follow me on Bookbub!
Click on the picture below – see the Follow button?

Made in the USA
Monee, IL
18 February 2021